The Firebird in Russian folklore is a fiery, illuminated bird; magical, iconic, coveted. Its feathers continue to glow when removed, and a single feather, it is said, can light up a room. Some who claim to have seen the Firebird say it even has glowing eyes. The Firebird is often the object of a quest. In one famous tale, the Firebird needs to be captured to prevent it from stealing the king's golden apples, a fruit bestowing youth and strength on those who partake of the fruit. But in other stories, the Firebird has another mission: it is always flying over the earth providing hope to any who may need it. In modern times and in the West, the Firebird has become part of world culture. In Igor Stravinsky's ballet *The Firebird*, it is a creature half-woman and half-bird, and the ballerina's role is considered by many to be the most demanding in the history of ballet.

The Overlook Press in the U.S. and Gerald Duckworth in the UK, in adopting the Firebird as the logo for its expanding Ardis publishing program, consider that this magical, glowing creature—in legend come to Russia from a faraway land—will play a role in bringing Russia and its literature closer to readers everywhere.

The Goatibex Constellation
Fazil Iskander

Translated by
Helen Burlingame

ARDIS PUBLISHERS
NEW YORK, NY

This edition first published in paperback in the United States and the United Kingdom in 2015 by Ardis Publishers, an imprint of Peter Mayer Publishers, Inc.

NEW YORK:
The Overlook Press
141 Wooster Street
New York, NY 10012
www.overlookpress.com
For bulk and special sales, please contact sales@overlookny.com,
or write us at the above address.

LONDON:
Gerald Duckworth & Co. Ltd.
30 Calvin Street
London E1 6NW
info@duckworth-publishers.co.uk
www.ducknet.co.uk
For bulk and special sales, please contact sales@duckworth-publishers.co.uk,
or write us at the above address.

Cataloging in Publication Data is available from the Library of Congress

A catalogue record for this book is available from the British Library

Printed in the United States of America
ISBN: 978-1-4683-1075-7 (US)
ISBN: 978-0-7156-5001-1 (UK)

2   4   6   8   10   9   7   5   3   1
Go to www.ardisbooks.com to read or download the latest Ardis catalog.

AUTHOR'S PREFACE

A certain Moscow publishing house once asked me to write an introduction for the Persian language edition of my short stories. I got to work on it, and what emerged was a story equal in length to those it was supposed to preface.

I don't know how this happened, though I may have been somewhat influenced by the fact that the introduction was to be paid for in the usual fashion—that is, according to the number of pages.

"A strange introduction," said the editorial assistant despondently as he took the manuscript in hand and began counting the pages. "Why, this is as much as a tenth of the whole book."

"There's a way to get around that," I suggested.

"How?" he asked, brightening.

"What's to prevent your increasing the overall size of the book, thus cutting down on the relative size of the introduction?"

"No," he replied, for some reason offended by my proposal, "our Persian readers would never forgive us for that."

"Well, suit yourself," I said, and without further delay set off for the accounting office to collect my fee for the introduction.

Not long ago I learned that the same publishing house was planning to bring out another foreign-language edition of my book. When I went to volunteer my services as author of the introduction, however, I was told that the rumors regarding the publication of my book were premature—from which I can only conclude that there must also be such a thing as mature rumors. I have since been informed by certain other sources that the book is actually going to be published, but for the time being the whole business remains a tightly guarded editorial secret.

I hope that the introduction to the American edition of *The Goatibex Constellation* will be considerably shorter than the Persian one, all the more so since it's length has not, as far as I know, been stipulated by the publisher.

And so, without further ado, what is a goatibex?

In one of our Abkhazian newspapers I once happened to read an article about a man who had crossed a female goat with a male ibex and produced a new animal which he called a goat-ibex. (Abkhazia, by the way, is my native land; it is situated on the Black Sea coast and is one of the most charming of our Soviet autonomous republics.)

According to the article, the goatibex was in good health and apparently was quite eager to overtake and even surpass the population figures of the more traditional breeds of livestock. Taking into account this and certain other unique characteristics of the hybrid (its high meat and wool yield, for example), the author of the article predicted an unprecedented leap in livestock production, all the more so since there could be no doubt as to the goatibex's jumping ability—the latter having been inherited from his male parent, the mountain-dwelling ibex.

Along with certain other digressions from the main theme, my story contains several reminiscences of my grandfather's house and an account of one of my childhood adventures. Why have I included these? Because in the course of writing about the mannequins of goatibexation I began to feel the need for a breath of fresh air. This need was a purely subjective one, but I decided to justify it artistically by letting these childhood memories intrude upon the main theme and overwhelm it with their poetic freshness and vigor.

The creative process is, of course, an unexplained phenomenon, and although we are able to separate some of the individual strands entering into the web of causality, these strands, taken by themselves, represent only a fraction of the whole.

On the subject of humor I also have a number of observations which I am ready to pass on free of charge. I have, to be sure, already shared these observations with my Persian readers, but after all, is it not the author's right and even obligation to seek out the widest possible audience for his views?

In order to attain a genuine sense of humor I believe one has to descend to the depths of pessimism. And only when one has peered into the murky abyss and convinced oneself that here too there is nothing, can one make one's way haltingly back from the abyss. The traces of this return trip will be humor—genuine humor.

Humor possesses one modest but undisputed virtue: it is always truthful. In fact, one can even go so far as to say that all humor is humorous precisely because it *is* truthful. Not every truth is humorous, of course, but all humor is truthful.

It is with this dubious aphorism that I should like to conclude my introduction to the American edition of *The Goatibex Constellation.*

FAZIL ISKANDER

The Goatibex
Constellation

I

One fine day I was fired from the editorial staff of a youth newspaper in Central Russia where I had been working for less than a year. I had been assigned to the paper directly after graduation from the Institute.

By some freakish coincidence it turned out that the paper's editor-in-chief wrote poetry, and what was worse, published his verse under a pseudonym. He had taken the pseudonym out of respect for the local authorities, although as it turned out he could have spared himself the trouble since the local authorities already knew about his verse. They kept this knowledge to themselves, however, having apparently decided that a weakness for poetry was quite forgivable in the editor of a youth newspaper.

The local authorities knew about his verse, but I did not. Thus it happened that at my very first staff meeting I began criticizing a certain poem which had recently appeared in our paper. Although I criticized the poem without in any way making fun of it, my voice may have betrayed a hint of condescension—the sort of Muscovite snobbishness which is perhaps understandable in a young man fresh out of a Moscow institute.

As I was speaking, I noticed a strange look pass over the faces of my colleagues. I attached no great importance to this, however, merely assuming that they were impressed by the smooth logic of my presentation.

Perhaps I might even have gotten away with my indiscretion, had it not been for one small detail. Passing himself off as a village Komsomol, the poet had spoken of the advantages of the potato digger over the manual harvesting of potatoes. In my spiritual and even literary naiveté I concluded that this was but

11

another one of those poems that are always finding their way into editorial offices all over the world. And not wishing to be overly harsh on the aspiring young poet, I concluded my speech with the comment that for a village Komsomol it was a fairly literate attempt.

Never again did I criticize our editor's poems. The damage had already been done, however, and after this he no longer trusted me. Apparently he assumed that I had merely shifted tactics and was now criticizing him behind his back.

All in all, he was probably right in concluding that one versifier was quite enough for a provincial youth newspaper. He had no doubts as to which one of us it was to be, nor for that matter did I.

A drive to cut back on personnel was launched that same spring, and I became one of its victims. Spring may be a good time for staff reductions, but it is a poor time for parting with one's sweetheart.

At the time I happened to be in love with a girl who spent her days working in the accounting office of one of our military installations, and her evenings attending night school. Between these two occupations she managed to schedule a number of rendezvous, and not only with me. She bestowed these rendezvous so liberally that it was as if she were making her way through life with an enormous bouquet of flowers, carelessly scattering them in every direction. Each recipient of one of these flowers considered himself the future owner of the whole bouquet, and as a result there arose a great many misunderstandings.

I remember one occasion in particular. She and I had met in the park and for some time had been strolling under the majestic old lindens which lined its paths. I gazed at her face, which kept flickering and dissolving in the twilight, and was entranced by the sound of her laughter. The leaves rustled beneath our feet, and music could be heard somewhere in the distance. It was a marvelous evening.

As we emerged from the path onto a well-lit intersection, I noticed a group of young men standing off to the side. One of them, the least friendly in appearance, abruptly abandoned his companions and began moving in our direction. I took an immediate dislike to his surly face, and it even occurred to me that I would have preferred to see someone else from the group approaching us. But he kept on advancing and when he finally reached us, suddenly, without uttering a word, he slapped her on the face. I pounced on him, and we began to struggle. But at this point the others came up and spoiled everything. Rather than letting us fight it out to the end, they knocked me down and gave me a good thrashing. Such, it seems, is the modern variant of the old-fashioned duel.

It turned out that she had made a date to meet him in this very spot at about this time.

"Well, okay, but why here, in the very same park where you're walking with me?" I asked, trying to fathom the logic of her behavior.

"I don't know," she laughed in reply as she gently brushed off my jacket. "But you'll have to admit that he managed to get even with me too."

I looked at her face and sorrowfully reflected that everything seemed to suit her. In fact, her face looked even prettier after the slap.

Shortly after this incident, she began to be pursued by a certain army major—an old man, as he seemed to us at the time. She would often joke about him, and this worried me. I had already observed that if a girl makes too much fun of her admirer and the latter is sufficiently persistent, she may end up marrying him, if only for the simple reason that he makes her laugh. And I had no doubts as to the major's persistence.

Needless to say, the foregoing circumstances did not greatly contribute to my creative output and eventually provided the editor with a pretext for ridding himself of an unwelcome competitor.

To avoid being accused of any bias in relation to me, he also fired our staff cleaning lady. Actually, he should have fired the two staff chauffeurs, who for the past month had had nothing to do anyway. As a result of a recent government economy drive on fuel they had been unable to get any gasoline, and now out of sheer laziness they had begun to grow beards and for days on end would sit around playing checkers on the office couch. As they sat there, too lazy to take off their coats, one saw in their sullenly bloated features the traces of a still lingering hangover.

And whereas in the past we would have jumped into the staff limousine and tracked down our story in a single day, now we ended up taking a three-or four-day business trip for the same story. The drive to cut back on business trips had not yet been launched.

Be that as it may, the staff reduction took place and I decided it was time to return to my native Abkhazia. Upon dismissal I received my regular month's salary, some sort of inexplicable vacation funds, and an additional fee for my most recent articles. This struck me as an altogether generous settlement, and I went away happy in the knowledge that my financial independence was fully assured for at least two months. At that time my notions of material well-being were still those of a student.

The day of my departure finally arrived, and I was escorting my girlfriend to class for the last time.

"Be sure to write," she said. Then, flashing one last, dazzling smile in my direction, she disappeared into the dark recesses of the night school.

Though I knew that a love such as ours exists independently of time or place, still, I was somewhat stung by her fortitude. I would have preferred a more tangible proof of her affection than that dazzling smile.

I spent the evening on a damp park bench, reflecting on the past and dreaming of the future that lay before me. As I was sitting there in that cold, bare, but already blossoming park, I suddenly heard Grieg's "Solvejg-Song" pouring forth from the loudspeaker. Moved by this beautiful music, I was able for the moment, and with the merest trace of self-deception, to endow my beloved with all of Solvejg's spiritual qualities.

No, I thought, whatever its inadequacies, a world that can produce a song such as this has every right to happiness and will be happy.

But enough of such daydreaming, I thought to myself. Instead of sitting here, you should be helping to improve the world. It's high time you grew up, high time you found a job with a real, adult newspaper where people are concerned with real, adult issues.

Here I should point out that even before my dismissal I had for some time been thoroughly fed up with the pseudo-youth vocabulary of our paper and its constant bursts of empty enthusiasm.

I was fed up with its slick contrivance in place of creativity, its "deep" talk instead of depth, and its vivaciousness instead of vitality. In short, a damned, lousy newspaper!

But every cloud has a silver lining, I thought to myself. Now you're going to become a real journalist, and she will understand and appreciate you. What exactly she was supposed to understand, I was not quite sure, but that she would appreciate me, I did not doubt for a moment.

Later that evening some of my friends accompanied me to the railroad station. Warmed by their affectionate farewells, I departed for Moscow where I was to make a brief stopover before rushing home to my native land, to the enchanted South.

While in Moscow I managed to have one of my poems published—no small feat in those days and one which helped me to get even with my former editor, whose poems were *not* published in Moscow. In addition, my poem was to serve as a sort of calling card heralding my arrival at *Red Subtropics*, the Abkhazian newspaper where I hoped to find a job.

II

"Yes, yes, we've already read it," exclaimed Avtandil Avtandilovich, the editor-in-chief of *Red Subtropics,* as he caught sight of me in the corridor of the editorial office. "By the way, don't you ever plan to come back here for good?"

Apparently he thought that I had merely come home on vacation.

"Yes, I'm considering it," I replied, and right then and there we came to an agreement. He agreed to hire me as soon as a certain elderly staff member retired.

I spent the next month wandering along the city's deserted beaches, trying to put my not very happy reflections into verse. She had not answered either of my two letters, and pride prevented me from writing a third. I did, however, write to one of my friends at the youth newspaper, making casual reference to the fact that I had gotten a job with a genuine, adult newspaper. I asked him to drop me a line in care of the paper whenever he had a chance. And by the way, I added, if you happen to run into a certain someone, and if the subject should happen to come up, you can tell her about my new job. In closing, I asked him to convey my best regards to everyone in the office, the editor included. The tone of the letter was, I think, calm and dignified, with perhaps a slight overlay of worldly condescension.

The air of my native land, saturated with the sharp aroma of the sea and with the soft, feminine fragrance of blooming wisteria, gradually soothed and comforted me. Perhaps the iodine dissolved in the sea air has a healing effect on emotional as well as physical wounds. At any rate, for days at a time I lay sunbathing on the beach, which was still deserted except for a few young men who would occasionally stroll past in small groups. These local

16

Don Juans would cast a proprietary eye over the entire beach, studying its terrain like a general scrutinizing the site where momentous battles are soon to take place.

The man who was supposed to retire finally agreed to do so, not because he wanted to, but because a campaign had recently been launched to encourage people of retirement age actually to retire. In the past he had always tried to make light of his age, but now he was more or less forced to give in. His colleagues gave him a festive farewell and even presented him with an inflatable rubber boat. Although he had also hinted at some fancy fishing tackle, no one had caught the hint; the inflatable boat alone was enough to bankrupt our union treasury. Later on he began telling everyone that he had been made to retire against his will and had even been deprived of his promised fishing tackle. Of course this was all utter nonsense. He had been promised an inflatable boat and had gotten it; but as for the fishing tackle, it had not even been mentioned.

I go into all this in such detail because to a certain extent it looked as if I were the one who was taking his place. Actually, however, the terms of my employment were different from his, since I was being hired as a local employee for whom no apartment would have to be provided.

I had been acquainted with the paper's editorial staff since my student days when during summer vacations at home I had tried to interest them in some of my poems. While my efforts in this direction had met with little success, I *had* learned something about the staff members themselves. Among other things, I knew for a fact that the paper's editor-in-chief, Avtandil Avtandilovich, had never written a poem in his life and had no intention of doing so. In fact, during the whole period of his employment with the paper he had to the best of my knowledge never written anything at all.

Avtandil Avtandilovich was a born leader and man of many talents. Like most Abkhazians he had a natural gift for making speeches and toasts. Not only was he an expert at the banquet table, but his height, curly hair and masculine appearance made his presence equally desirable and even indispensable at important meetings and conferences. He spoke all of the Caucasian languages fluently, and his toasts never had to be translated.

Before his editorial post he had headed a local industry— naturally, one on a scale appropriate to our small, but charming, autonomous Republic. Apparently he had managed the industry quite well—perhaps even too well, since the need had arisen to promote him, and when the opportunity presented itself, he was made editor-in-chief of the city newspaper.

As a man of great ability and resourcefulness he quickly mastered this new enterprise. His operational talents were truly phenomenal. Editorials would frequently appear in our paper on the very same day as in the Moscow papers, and sometimes even a day earlier.

As I had hoped, I was assigned to the paper's agricultural section. This was a period of radical reform for Soviet agriculture. Experiments were taking place right and left, and I wanted to see for myself what was going on, find out what it was all about, and eventually become an expert in my own right.

The paper's agricultural section was headed by Platon Samsonovich. If one wonders at the name, I should point out that in our region such names are as plentiful as fish in the sea. Apparently they are a holdover from the Greek and Roman colonization of the Black Sea coast.

I was already acquainted with Platon Samsonovich and had often gone fishing with him in the past. He was a quiet, peaceful individual and one of the most capable and experienced fishermen I had ever run across.

By the time I came to work for him, however, Platonov Samsonovich had completely changed. Not only had he lost all interest in fishing, but he had even sold his small boat. Gone too was his former peaceful exterior. With pursed lips and a certain purposeful glitter in his gloomy eyes, he would pace feverishly from one end of the office to the other. He had always been on the short side, but now he seemed to have shriveled up completely. He had grown even wirier than before and was absolutely charged with energy.

The cause of this sudden transformation was the goatibex-breeding campaign which had recently been launched in our region. Platon Samsonovich had initiated this campaign and was its main promoter.

Some two years before, Platon Samsonovich had paid a visit to one of our mountain game preserves and come back with a short news item on a certain breeding specialist who had succeeded in crossing a mountain ibex with a common goat. As a result of his experiment there appeared the world's first goatibex. Grazing peacefully among a herd of goats, the new animal could hardly suspect the glorious future that awaited it.

No one paid any attention to Platon Samsonovich's article—no one, that is, except for a certain very important individual who always spent his vacations at Cape Orange on the shores of our Republic. This individual, who was not exactly a minister but no less important than a minister, read the article and, upon reading it, exclaimed, "An interesting undertaking, to say the least."

At this point it would be difficult to ascertain whether he addressed these words to anyone in particular or merely uttered aloud the first thought that came into his head. In any case, the very next day Avtandil Avtandilovich received a phone call and was told by the voice at the other end of the receiver, "Our congratulations, Avtandil Avtandilovich. *He* said it's an interesting undertaking, to say the least."

Avtandil Avtandilovich promptly called a staff meeting and in an atmosphere of general rejoicing expressed his gratitude to Platon Samsonovich. At the same time he instructed the latter along with our staff photographer to set off immediately for the game preserve and this time to bring back a full-length article on the life and habits of the goatibex.

"It's not beyond the realm of possibility that the goatibex will some day play a significant role in our national economy," declared Avtandil Avtandilovich.

A week later our paper published a feature article entitled "An Interesting Undertaking, to Say the Least." The article took up a whole half page and was supplemented by two large photographs of the goatibex. Seen in profile, the animal's lower lip seemed to curl skeptically to the side, like that of some decadent aristocrat. In the second photograph the goatibex was shown fullface with his powerful and splendidly curved horns. Here his expression seemed to be one of bewilderment, as if he himself could not decide who he really was and which was better: to become a goat or remain an ibex.

The article gave a detailed account of the animal's daily food requirements and of his touching devotion to humans. His superiority to the common domestic goat was particularly stressed.

Fazil Iskander

First of all, it was pointed out that the average weight of the goat-ibex was twice that of the common goat—a circumstance of no little importance in light of the country's chronic meat shortages. Secondly, the goatibex was blessed with strong legs and a hardy constitution, and hence should be able to graze on the steepest mountain slopes almost without risk. Thanks, moreover, to his calm and gentle disposition, the animal would be easy to care for and a single goatherd should be able to tend as many as two thousand goatibexes.

The author adopted a somewhat lighter tone in his description of the goatibex's wool yield. The animals' thick wool of white and ashen hues was in his words a real bonus for the consumer industry. It seemed that the breeding specialist's wife had already knitted herself a sweater of goatibex wool—a garment which according to Platon Samsonovich was in no way inferior to any import. "Our fashion-conscious ladies will be satisfied," he declared.

It was further pointed out that the goatibex had inherited the jumping ability of his illustrious forebear, the ibex, as well as the latter's beautiful horns. If suitably processed, these horns could be used as decorations for the home or as attractive souvenirs for tourists and well-wishing foreign guests.

Platon Samsonovich had put heart and soul into this article, and to this day it stands out in my mind as the most colorful of the many articles devoted to the goatibex. And I have read all of them!

The article must have provoked considerable public response, for soon afterward our paper began to feature two new columns under the headings: "On the Trail of the Goatibex" and "Laughing at the Skeptics." All favorable letters were published with suitable commentary in the first column; any skeptical or critical letters appeared in the second column and were promptly attacked and repudiated.

Under the heading "On the Trail of the Goatibex" there was published a letter from a certain Moscow scientist* who declared

---

* What follows is an ironic fictional portrait of the Soviet biologist and agriculturalist Trofim D. Lysenko (1898–1976). Using the name of the famous Russian horticulturalist Michurin (1855–1935), Lysenko was able to impose his theory of "the inheritance of acquired characteristics" on the Soviet scientific community from the late forties until some years after Stalin's death. While Lysenko was to remain a powerful figure throughout the Khrushchev era, by the early sixties other more widely-accepted views on genetics were once again able to be heard. *(Translator's note.)*

that he personally was not at all surprised by the appearance of the goatibex, since all of this had long ago been foreseen by the followers of the Michurin school of biology. Certain other scientists, however, who had been captivated by theories of dubious validity, *had not* and naturally *could not* have foreseen anything of the sort. The great scientist concluded his letter with the statement that the appearance of the goatibex had helped to confirm the validity of his own experiments.

This individual was our country's most renowned scientist. In his day he had advanced the hypothesis that the ram is nothing other than a direct descendant of the prehistoric reptile which, in keeping with Darwin's teachings, had undergone a gradual transformation in its struggle for survival. The proof of his hypothesis had been based, it seems, on a comparative analysis of the frontal sinuses of the ram and the skull of an Assyrian reptile fossil.

On the basis of this analysis the great scientist logically concluded that the stubby tail of the ram—being in fact a vestigial reptile tail—ought still to have the capacity to revert to its original form. It remained only to develop this capacity while at the same time training the organism to cast off its present tail in some relatively painless fashion. This is precisely what the great scientist had been working on in recent years and, as far as one could tell, his experiments were meeting with some success.

There were, it is true, certain envious individuals who complained that no one had been able to repeat the great man's ingenious experiments. Such complaints were countered, however, with the quite sensible reply that what made these experiments ingenious was precisely the fact that they could *not* be repeated.

All this notwithstanding, the great scientist's support of our goatibex was both timely and beneficial.

In the same column a letter was published from one of our lady readers. Apparently she had not understood a word of Platon Samsonovich's article or else was going merely on hearsay, since she wished to find out where she could purchase a sweater made of goatibex wool. The editors politely informed her that although it was a bit premature to be discussing the commercial manufacture of sweaters, her letter did nonetheless provide food for thought. In fact, some of our manufacturing organizations should begin to make immediate preparations for the eventual stocking and processing of goatibex wool.

Under the same heading there also appeared a letter from the workers' collective of the city slaughterhouse. The workers wished to congratulate the agricultural toilers on their interesting new undertaking and to offer their services to whichever kolkhoz became the first to specialize in goatibex breeding.

In the second column, "Laughing at the Skeptics," excerpts were published from the letters of a certain livestock expert and an agronomist.

The livestock expert politely expressed his doubts as to the hybrid's ability to reproduce itself, thus calling into question the whole future of the goatibex venture. In this connection, however, the editorial board was happy to report that the goatibex had already impregnated eight female goats and according to all indications had no intention of stopping here. The impregnated goats were all in good health and the mating continued.

The agronomist proved to be more acrimonious. He made fun of each and every one of the goatibex's qualities, from the first to the last and all of them as a whole. The animal's jumping ability was an object of particular derision. I should like to know, he wrote, how our collective farmers can possibly benefit from the goatibex's jumping ability. As if we didn't have trouble enough with the jumping ability of our own goats and the damage they do to our corn fields—now you want to saddle us with the goatibex! After this he went on to make some wisecrack about the possibility of our paper's entering the goatibex as a contestant for the high jump at the next Olympic games.

The agronomist's letter was given a worthy rebuff by Platon Samsonovich. He began by calmly explaining that the goatibex's jumping ability was in fact a great asset, since future herds of goatibexes would be able to graze on high alpine meadows inaccessible to the common domestic goat. And there, thanks to his great jumping ability, the animal would be able to escape with relative ease from the predators which continued to prey on our communal livestock.

As for the jumping ability of our collective farm goats, here the editorial board could take no responsibility. All responsibility for the goats lay with the collective farm shepherds, most of whom probably spent their days sleeping or playing cards. Such shepherds should be fined, and not only the shepherds but the kolkhoz leadership as well—from the chairman on down through those agronomists who were unable to distinguish between alpine meadows and Olympic fields.

Platon Samsonovich's reply apparently silenced the acrimonious agronomist for good. The polite livestock expert, however, continued to make himself heard, and once again his name appeared in the column "Laughing at the Skeptics."

He declared that the paper's reply had not convinced him, since even if the hybrid did have the capacity to mate with female goats, this did not necessarily mean that any offspring would be forthcoming. Moreover, he felt that the livestock industry should be placing its main emphasis on the larger breeds of cattle (on the buffalo in particular), rather than on the goatibex which, while larger than the goat, was nonetheless a small breed.

In reply to this letter Platon Samsonovich stated that, quite to the contrary, the goatibex's mating capacity did indeed prove that he would be able to reproduce himself. In a very few months we shall see for ourselves; time is on our side, wrote Platon Samsonovich.

As for the proper course to be adopted by the livestock industry, here he had two points to make. First of all, even though the goatibex was smaller than the large breeds of cattle, it could by no means be called a small breed. And secondly, the livestock expert's excessive preoccupation with the larger breeds of cattle clearly demonstrated that he was still suffering from the gigantomania characteristic of the period of the personality cult—a period which had come and gone, never to return.

Several months later the paper devoted a whole page to the observance of a joyful event. All of the thirteen she-goats impregnated by the goatibex had given birth; of these, four had brought forth twins, while one of them had actually produced triplets.

An enormous photograph depicting the goatibex along with his harem and young offspring ran the full width of the page. The goatibex stood in the center, and this time his face did not express the slightest bewilderment. He seemed to have found himself, and his appearance was calm and dignified.

Fazil Iskander

By the time I came to work for *Red Subtropics*, Platon Sam-sonovich had become the paper's leading reporter. No longer confining himself to agricultural issues, he now dealt with cultural and educational matters as well, and even wrote editorials for the propaganda section. In fact, his article "The Goatibex as a Weapon for Antireligious Propaganda" had been singled out as one of the paper's best articles of the year.

And now, for days on end, Platon Samsonovich would sit at his desk, surrounded by biology texts, letters from breeding specialist and all sorts of diagrams. Sometimes he would grow thoughtful and suddenly wince.

"What's the matter, Platon Samsonovich?" I would ask.

"You know," he would reply, now reverting to his former cheerful and lively self, "I often think back to my first article. Why, at the time I actually wondered whether the item was worth turning in. To think that I almost let this great undertaking slip through my fingers!"

"Well, and what if you had?" I would ask.

"Don't even suggest such a thing," he would answer, wincing once again.

Platon Samsonovich devoted all his time and energy to the newspaper. He was always the first to arrive in the morning and the last to leave at night. In fact, such was his zeal and dedication that I, his assistant, felt almost embarrassed to leave the office at the end of a normal work-day. He never seemed to mind, however, and was probably just as happy to be left alone. He was unable to work at home, since his apartment consisted of only one room, which he shared with his wife and several grown children. Years before, he had applied to the city soviet for a new apartment, but only now, some weeks after my arrival, was his request finally granted. No doubt his rise to fame in connection with the goatibex had more than a little to do with the Soviet's decision.

We all congratulated him on the acquisition of his new apartment and even hinted at the possibility of a housewarming. For some unknown reason, however, he obstinately ignored our hints.

It was not until several days later that we discovered the reason for his obstinacy. It turned out that he had left his family and was staying on in the old apartment. Apparently he had tried

24

to leave home several times before, but without success—first of all because he had no place to go, and secondly because his wife had immediately gone to complain to the editor, who on each occasion had managed to persuade him to return to the fold.

On this occasion too Platon Samsonovich's wife went straight to the editor and demanded, "Give me back my inventor."

Avtandil Avtandilovich summoned Platon Samsonovich to his office and began trying to persuade him as usual. This time, however, Platon Samsonovich stood his ground and flatly refused to return to his family, although he was willing to help in their financial support.

"Times have changed," said Avtandil Avtandilovich to the wife, "you'll have to handle your family affairs by yourself…"

"They're always making fun of me," Platon Samsonovich is supposed to have interjected at this point.

"What do you mean, making fun of you?" asked the editor in surprise. Then turning to the wife, he added: "Platon Samsonovich is working on an important national problem…"

"They're always interfering with my thought processes," Platon Samsonovich is supposed to have prompted.

"Give me back my inventor," repeated the wife.

"She's making fun of me even now," complained Platon Samsonovich.

"It isn't as if he were asking for a divorce," said the editor.

"That's all I need!" exclaimed the wife.

"Just think of him as living in his own private office," concluded Avtandil Avtandilovich.

"But what are people going to think?" asked the wife after a moment's reflection.

With that it was settled. Platon Samsonovich was not, of course, leaving his family in order to acquire a new one, much less a mistress. Rather it was as if he were removing himself from all worldly cares in order to devote himself wholeheartedly to his favorite cause.

Despite his partial desertion Platon Samsonovich's wife regularly returned to the old apartment to tidy things up and to supply her husband with fresh linen. For his part Platon Samsonovich continued to work on his brainchild—now with twice as much energy as before—and from time to time would discover a new vantage point from which to view the problems of goatibex breeding.

When a new soft drink pavilion was opened next to one of our seaside cafés, he managed to have it named "The Watering Place of the Goatibex." He was a frequent visitor to the new establishment, and sometimes in the evening when emerging from the cafe, I would see him sitting there, sipping our Caucasian mineral water Narzan with his arms resting on the counter, and on his face the look of a weary but contented patron.

Although Platon Samsonovich was in favor of promoting the goatibex in the most surprising and varied ways, he would not tolerate any levity in this connection. Thus, for example, when our paper's humorist compared a certain polygamist and incorrigible defaulter in his alimony payments to the goatibex, Platon Samsonovich stood up at a staff meeting and declared that such a comparison only served to discredit an important national undertaking in the eyes of our collective farm workers.

"Though no one should be accused of any political error, still Platon Samsonovich's point is well taken," concluded Avtandil Avtandilovich in a conciliatory tone.

Platon Samsonovich had worked out an appropriate diet for the goatibex and was now urging our collective farmers to follow it. Wishing at the same time to leave some room for individual initiative, he suggested that they try supplementing his diet with various foods of their own choice and report their findings to the newspaper.

"Well, this is a real breakthrough!" he exclaimed to me one day as he approached my desk with a popular Moscow magazine in his hand, and pointed lovingly at its cover. Glancing up, I saw a photograph of the goatibex with his entire family—the same photograph which had appeared in our paper, only here it was in color and looked even more festive.

Shortly afterwards one of the Moscow newspapers ran an article entitled "An Interesting Undertaking, to Say the Least" which told of our Republic's innovative experiments in goatibex breeding. The paper advised the collective farmers of the central and black earth regions of the country to study and follow our innovative example—without excessive panic and without overdoing it, but at the same time without any costly delays.

Wisely anticipating any objections which might be raised with regard to climatic differences between the Caucasus and other regions farther to the north, the author of the article reminded his readers that the goatibex would hardly suffer from the cold, since on his father's side he had been raised in the high alpine meadows of the Caucasian mountains.

Platon Samsonovich was quietly exultant. At our last staff meeting only a few days before, he had announced rather precipitously that it was time to challenge the State of Iowa, our competitor in the production of corn, to compete with us in goatibex breeding.

"But they don't even raise goatibexes," objected Avtandil Avtandilovich, though not without a shade of uncertainty in his voice.

"Well, just let them try and see how they do under their private enterprise system," replied Platon Samsonovich.

"I'll have to consult some colleagues on this," said Avtandil Avtandilovich. Then by way of indicating that the meeting was adjourned, he switched on his office fan.

This fan stood on a table directly across from his desk and he would always turn it off at the beginning of each meeting. At such moments, with his head rising directly above the greasy blades of the fan, he looked like a pilot who had just flown in from distant parts. Later on, upon closing the meeting, he would once again switch on the fan and his face would tense, as if he were about to lift off.

The day after the meeting Platon Samsonovich was informed by the editor that he would have to wait as far as the State of Iowa was concerned.

"Just between us, he's one of these play-it-safe types," Platon Samsonovich later confided to me, nodding in the direction of the editor's office.

Under the heading "On the Trail of the Goatibex" there once appeared a letter from the staff members of an agricultural research institute in Ciscaucasia. They reported that they had been following our undertaking with interest and had themselves already crossed a Ciscaucasian ibex with a common goat. The first ibexigoat was reported to be in excellent health and growing by leaps and bounds.

Writing on behalf of all the goatibex fans in Transcaucasia, Platon Samsonovich congratulated our northern colleagues on their great success and predicted that they would be even more successful in the future if they continued to stick to the diet which he had worked out for the new animal. He concluded by declaring that he had always known it would be they, the Ciscaucasians—our brothers and closest neighbors to the north, who would be the first to follow our lead in this new undertaking.

The letter from Ciscaucasia was printed verbatim except that in place of the word "ibexigoat" Platon Samsonovich substituted the term "goatibex" adopted by us.

For some reason or other the authors of the letter were offended by this harmless correction and shortly thereafter sent a letter of protest to the editor in which they stated that they had never even considered feeding their ibexigoat according to our diet, but were feeding and would continue to feed it strictly according to the diet worked out by their own professional staff. In addition, they felt obliged to point out that the term "goatibex" was completely unscientific. The very fact (and facts cannot be denied!) that it was a male ibex which was crossed with a female goat, and not vice versa, clearly indicated the predominance of the ibex over the goat—a circumstance which should, of course, be reflected in the animal's name if one were to approach the matter with scientific precision.

The term "goatibex," they went on, would be justified only if one succeeded in crossing a male goat with a female ibex, and even this would be stretching things a bit. In such a case, however, there would be no further grounds for argument since we would be dealing with two different animals produced by two different means, a situation which would naturally justify the use of different names. In any case, you can go on experimenting with your goatibexes if you wish, but we for our part will continue in the future, as we have in the past, to stick to our ibexigoats.

Such was the general tone and content of the letter from our colleagues in Ciscaucasia.

"We'll have to print it; they *are* specialists, after all," said Avtandil Avtandilovich as he handed the letter to Platon Samsonovich. Apparently he had considered it of sufficient importance to deliver in person.

Platon Samsonovich quickly scanned the letter and then threw it down on the desk.

"Well, only if it goes in the 'Laughing at the Skeptics' column," he said.

"We can't do that," objected Avtandil Avtandilovich. "These are specialists expressing their opinion. And besides, you did take liberties with their first letter."

"The whole country knows about the goatibex," protested Platon Samsonovich, "but no one's even heard of the ibexigoat."

"That's true," agreed Avtandil Avtandilovich, "and the Moscow press did use our name.... But where did you get the idea that they were using our diet?"

"What other diet could they be using?" retorted Platon Samsonovich, shrugging his shoulders. "Up to now, everyone's been using our diet..."

"Well, all right," agreed Avtandil Avtandilovich after a moment's reflection, "write up an intelligent reply, and we'll present both items in the form of a friendly debate."

"I'll have it ready today," exclaimed Platon Samsonovich, perking up at the very thought. He reached for a red pencil and took the specialists' letter in hand.

Avtandil Avtandilovich left the office.

"The schoolboy's trying to out-teach the teacher," muttered Platon Samsonovich, nodding his head so vaguely that I was not sure whether he was referring to the editor or to his unexpected opponents from the north.

Several days later the two items appeared in the newspaper. Platon Samsonovich's reply was entitled "To Our Colleagues beyond the Mountains" and written in an aggressive spirit. He began with a distant analogy. Just as America was discovered by Columbus, but given the name America in honor of the adventurer Amerigo Vespucci who, as everyone knows, did *not* discover America, so, in similar fashion, wrote Platon Samsonovich, our Ciscaucasian colleagues are trying to give their name to someone else's creation.

When we corrected the awkward and imprecise name "ibexigoat" in our colleagues' first letter by inserting the euphonious and universally-accepted term "goatibex," we assumed that they had merely made a slip of the pen—all the more so since the extremely naive and somewhat immature contents of the letter did not preclude the possibility of such a slip or even of a simple confusion of terms. We perceived all this at first glance, but printed the letter all the same, considering it our duty to support a still weak and hesitant but nonetheless purely motivated attempt to keep pace with the most advanced experiments of our time.

But what do we now find to be the case? It turns out that what we assumed to be a slip of the pen or a simple confusion of terms was actually the false and harmful manifestation of a whole system of beliefs. And since it is always the system itself one might fight, we hereby take up the gauntlet flung down from beyond the mountains.

Is it perhaps possible, continued Platon Samsonovich, that the name "ibexigoat," for all its clumsiness, may from the scientific point of view more accurately reflect the essence of the new creature? No, even here our colleagues from beyond the mountains have fallen wide of the mark. The real essence of the new creature is expressed precisely in the name "goatibex," since it is this name which accurately reflects the primacy of man over untamed nature. Thus it is the domestic goat, known even to the ancient Greeks, which, as the more advanced species, occupies first place in our variant, thereby reaffirming the principle that it is man who conquers nature and not vice versa—which would indeed be monstrous.

But perhaps the name "ibexigoat" is somehow in keeping with the best traditions of our own Michurin biology? Wrong again, colleagues from beyond the mountains! Taking as an example some of the new varieties of apples raised by Michurin, we find such names as Bellefleur-Kitaika and Kandil-Kitaika— names which our people have long accepted and approved of. Here, as in our case, the wild Chinese apple Kitaika occupies its altogether fitting and respectable second place.

As for the idea of crossing a female ibex with a male goat, continued Platon Samsonovich, this seems like a rather strange proposal to be coming from the mouths of specialists. In the first place, given the undesirably and even frighteningly large proportions of the female ibex, it is highly unlikely that a male goat would even attempt to mate with her. But even supposing such a union took place, what would we and the national economy have to gain from it? To answer this question we need only consult our own or foreign texts on the subject of mule breeding.

Centuries of experience in mule breeding have clearly demonstrated that the mating of a male horse with a female ass produces a hinny, whereas the more desirable mule results from the mating of a male ass with a female horse. As is well-known, the hinny is a weak, undeveloped and sickly animal which in addition has a tendency to bite. The mule, on the other hand, is an extremely useful animal and one which plays a worthy role in our national economy, especially in the economy of the southern republics. (The possibility of extending the area of mule breeding farther to the north and of raising even hardier species is not presently under consideration, though the impartial reader could learn a great deal from the ten-day mule run between Moscow and Leningrad which took place in the heart of winter with the animals harnessed to sleighs and hauling a full load [see the *Large Soviet Encyclopedia*, Volume XI, page 206]).

From the foregoing it should be perfectly clear that when produced by our time-tested method, the goatibex can and should be equated with the mule, whereas if produced in the manner suggested by our Ciscaucasian colleagues, he would turn out to be that very same hinny mentioned above. For this reason we can only reject the proposal of our Ciscaucasian colleagues as an attempt—perhaps an unintentional one, but an attempt nonetheless—to set our livestock-breeding industry onto the false paths of idealism.

Our colleagues from beyond the mountains seem to imply that our goatibexes are the deviants, and only their single ibexi-goat is keeping in step. But in step with whom?

The mysterious laconism of this last phrase had an ominous ring to it.

Some two weeks had passed and still we had no reply from the Ciscaucasians. For some reason or other they had chosen to keep silent, and this disturbed our editor no end.

"Perhaps their goatibex has died and now they're too embarrassed to continue the debate," suggested Platon Samsonovich.

"Well, call their institute and find out what's going on," ordered Avtandil Avtandilovich.

"But won't we be losing face if we call first?" objected Platon Samsonovich.

"On the contrary," replied Avtandil Avtandilovich, "it will only show how confident we are that we're in the right."

Platon Samsonovich placed his call and, having gotten through to the institute, was informed that the ibexigoat was alive and well, but that the staff members had decided to cut short the debate since only time would tell whose ibexigoats would be the first to prosper and multiply.

"Whose *goatibexes,*" corrected Platon Samsonovich before hanging up the receiver. "Nothing to say for themselves," he winked in my direction, and rubbing his hands in satisfaction, he returned to his desk.

I was very impatient to see a real, live goatibex with my own eyes. Much as he approved of my enthusiasm, however, Platon Samsonovich was in no hurry to send me off to the countryside. Up till then I'd had only one out-of-town assignment, and it had not been an unqualified success.

I had set out to sea at dawn with the leading brigade of a fishing collective located just beyond the city limits. Everything had been perfect: the lilac-colored sea, the old dory, and the fishermen themselves—strong, agile and indefatigable. But then, after they had made their haul and we were already on our way back, instead of taking the fish directly to the processing plant, they had veered toward a small promontory which lay off to our side. From along the shore some women with pails and baskets were making their way toward this same promontory, and I could see that we were fated to meet.

"Hey, fellows, do you really think we should stop here?" I asked, perhaps a bit belatedly, since the bow of the dory had just touched shore.

"Sure we should," they cheerfully assured me, and right away the bargaining was off to a lively start. Within fifteen minutes all of the fish had been traded for rubles and a variety of home-grown produce.

When we set out to sea once again, I tried to lecture them on the impropriety of what they had done. They listened politely but went right on laying out the food and slicing the fresh bread. The meal was soon ready, and when they asked me to join them, I naturally accepted. Anything else would have been unspeakably rude.

We ate our fill, polished off a bottle or two, and immediately afterwards fell into a deep, untroubled sleep.

Later that same day the men explained to me that there had been too few fish to bother with. The processing plant would not even have accepted such a small quantity and, in any case, they were sure to exceed their quota for the season.

Realizing that none of this was proper material for an article, I resigned myself to writing a "Ballad of the Fishing Industry," in which I celebrated the fisherman's labor without being too specific as to how he profited from the fruits of his labor. The ballad was well received in the editorial office and soon appeared in print as a new and sophisticated newspaper genre.

But to return to the goatibex.

A regional conference was currently being organized for the purpose of discussing common problems and experiences in goatibex breeding. The animals had already been apportioned among the most prosperous kolkhozes in order that their mass reproduction might begin, but unfortunately, certain kolkhoz chairmen had tried to wangle their way out of the new venture with the excuse that for years they had not even raised goats, much less goatibexes. Such individuals were put to shame, however, and eventually forced to purchase appropriate numbers of female goats. But no sooner had the goats been purchased than our paper began receiving complaints to the effect that some of the goatibexes were acting very cooly toward the females. This prompted our editor to suggest the possibility of artificial insemination, but Platon Samsonovich was firmly opposed to the idea, insisting that such a compromise would only play into the hands of the lazier chairmen. The coolness of the goatibex, he declared, was but a reflection of the kolkhoz chairmen's own coolness to everything new.

It was just at this time that we received a letter from an anonymous kolkhoz worker in the village of Walnut Springs who was writing in to complain about his chairman's disgraceful treatment of the goatibex. In addition to depriving the animal of adequate food and shelter, this chairman had actually set dogs on it. The kolkhoz workers were moved to tears by the sufferings of the new animal, but were too afraid of the chairman to protest.

The anonymous letter concluded with the words: "Yours sincerely, in a spirit of righteous indignation."

"He may be exaggerating, of course," said Platon Samsonovich as he showed me the letter, "but where there's smoke, there's fire. So I'd like you to go out to Walnut Springs and see for yourself what's going on."

He paused for a moment and then added, "I know this chairman; his name is Illarion Maximovich. He's a pretty good manager, but a real conservative; he thinks of nothing but his tea crop."

"As for the general line of your article," continued Platon Samsonovich, now extending his hand into the air as if groping for the contours of my future article, "it should run pretty much as follows: 'Tea is fine, but the meat and wool of the goatibex are even better.' "

"Okay," I replied.

"Remember," he said, stopping me as I was halfway through the door, "a lot will depend on this assignment."

"I understand."

Platon Samsonovich reflected for a moment.

"There was something else I wanted to tell you.... Oh yes, be sure you get up in time to make the morning bus."

"Now really, Platon Samsonovich!" I exclaimed and with that was off to fill out my travel voucher.

On the way I stopped off at the mail and supply room and picked up a notebook, two pencils (just in case I should lose my pen), and a penknife with which to sharpen them. Nothing was to be left to chance!

III

The bus sped smoothly and powerfully along the highway. On the right side of the road, beyond the green gardens and small white houses, one could catch a glimpse of the sea, which looked warm even from the distance. It seemed to be saturated with a soothing abundance of summer heat and of swimmers—mostly girls.

On our left green foothills drifted by, covered with fields of ripening corn and tangerine trees. Every once in a while one also saw fields of lop-eared little tung trees dotted with clusters of fruit.

During the war the soldiers of a construction battalion stationed in these parts had picked and eaten the fruit of the tung tree, which looks something like unripe apples but in fact is terribly poisonous. They had been strictly forbidden to touch the fruit, but they ate it anyway. These were hungry times, of course, and probably they thought the poisonous business had been dreamed up just to scare them. Usually it was enough to pump out their stomachs, though there were instances where the poisoning was fatal.

At times a light breeze—so unexpected that it seemed to have been stirred up by the bus itself as it rounded the curve—would bring with it a distant scent of musty fern, of sunbaked manure, and the milky fragrance of ripening corn. In all of this there was something so sweetly and sadly reminiscent of my childhood, of the village and my native land, that I could not help asking myself why it is that smells wield such great power over us. Why is it that there is no memory which can evoke the past with such intensity as the familiar smells which we associate with it? Perhaps the secret lies in their uniqueness—in the fact that we

35

cannot recall a smell in the absence of the smell itself or, in other words, cannot recreate it in our imagination. And when a smell is recreated in its natural form, it forces to the surface everything that was once associated with it. Visual and auditory impressions, on the other hand, are so frequently evoked through memory that perhaps for this very reason they eventually become dulled.

The passengers rode along on their soft, springy seats, rocking gently to the motion of the bus. The top of the bus was covered with a tinted-blue glass which turned the already blue sky into an incredibly rich and intense shade of blue. It was as if the glass were showing the sky how it should look, and the passengers how to look at it.

This particular bus had been turned over to the Public Transportation Office only recently. In the past it had transported foreign tourists around the city, and sometimes I used to catch a glimpse of it parked in front of the Botanical Gardens, the old fortress or some other scenic spot.

On this occasion it was filled with kolkhoz women on their way home from the city. Each of them carried a tightly stuffed bag or basket from which protruded the invariable cluster of *bubliki*-thick, ring-shaped rolls. Not without pride some of them also clasped Chinese thermos bottles, which reminded one simultaneously of a prize sports cup and an artillery shell.

Whole mountain ranges drifted slowly by on our left. The highest and most distant of them were covered with the first snow of the season, and their peaks glistened brightly against the horizon. The snow must have fallen the previous night, since these peaks had been bare the day before.

The mountains closer to us were covered with forests and shaded a dark blue. They were a long way away from the snow-covered peaks.

Suddenly, at a turn in the road and on a level with these closer mountains I saw a ridge of bare rocks. At the sight of them my heart contracted with fear and delight, for just below lay our village. As a child I had found these rocks terribly sinister and mysterious and had never ventured up to them, even though they were quite close—along a difficult route, to be sure. And now, reflecting on all the places I had been in my life, I suddenly regretted that I had never once visited these rocks.

Every summer from earliest childhood I had spent several months at my grandfather's house in the village. And always when I was up there in the mountains, I felt homesick—not so much for home itself as for the city. How I longed to return to the city and inhale once again that peculiarly city smell of dust fused with the odor of gasoline and rubber. I find it difficult to understand now, but in those days I would gaze nostalgically in the direction of the setting sun, comforted by the knowledge that our city lay there to the west, just beyond the soft and rounded contours of the mountain. And all the while I would be counting the days till the end of vacation.

Then, when we would finally return home to the city, I remember the sensation of extraordinary lightness in my legs as I took my first joyful steps on the asphalt pavement. At the time, I attributed this sensation to the smoothness of paved city streets, but it was probably due more than anything else to my endless walks along mountain paths, to the fresh air of the mountains, and to the simple and nutritious food we ate in the village.

Nowadays, no matter where I am, I never feel a trace of that eager and joyous longing for the city. On the contrary, I have begun to miss my grandfather's house more and more. Perhaps this is because I can no longer return to it: the old people have passed away and all their children have moved to the city, or at least closer to it. But in those years when the house still belonged to our family I was always too busy to spend much time there. It was as if I were keeping it in reserve, to be visited sometime in the future. And now that there's no one there to visit, I cannot help feeling deprived, as if I had somehow been cut off from my roots.

Even though I seldom visited my grandfather's house, it helped me from afar by its very existence. The smoke from its hearth, the generous shade of its trees—everything about it made me bolder and more self-confident. I was almost invulnerable because a part of my life, my roots, lived and thrived in the mountains. And when a man is aware of his roots and has some sense of continuity in his life, he can direct it more wisely and generously. And it is harder to rob or deprive him, because not all of his wealth is carried on his person.

I miss my grandfather's house with its large green yard. And I miss the old apple tree, long overgrown with a hardy grapevine, and the walnut tree under whose green canopy we would lie stretched out on a tanned ox or ibex hide during the hottest part of the day.

How many unripe apples we shook from the old apple tree, and how many unripe walnuts with their delicate kernels and thick, green skins not yet hardened into shells.

I miss the large, roomy kitchen of my grandfather's house, with its earthen floor, its warm, broad hearth and the long, heavy bench placed in front of the hearth. It was here that we would sit in the evenings, listening to endless tales of hunting expeditions, of treasures unearthed in ancient fortresses, and of our own fearless mountaineers who fought against the Russian tsars. On this same bench my uncle would sit cutting tobacco with his sharp hatchet. After a while he would seize a burning coal from the hearth and throw it into a heap of freshly cut tobacco. Then, with slow satisfaction he would stoke this smoking heap, making sure that it became thoroughly dried and saturated with the sweet aroma of wood smoke.

I miss the women's evening calls from hilltop to hilltop, from valley to mountain, and from mountain to valley. How lonely and pure is the sound of a woman's voice in the cool of the evening!

Just before sunset the chickens would remind us that they had, after all, been born to fly. First they would begin their restless cackling; then, eyeing the branches of the fig tree, they would suddenly fly upward, only to miss their mark and fall back to earth. After a second try they would finally reach the desired branch and settle in place behind the angrily squawking golden rooster.

At about this time my aunt would come out from the kitchen with a pail clanging in her hand. She would cross the yard with a light, nimble gait, stopping on her way to pick up a dry branch with which to chase away the calf. As she approached the cow pen, she would be greeted by questioning moos, while from under the elevated corn granary the baby goats would be heard, as noisy and playful as schoolchildren.

Before long Grandfather or one of the other men would appear with the rest of the goats, driving them home from pasture. Herded together in a noisy throng, the goats would come pouring into the yard, their stomachs bulging curiously to one side. Full of good spirits, the males would rear up on their hind legs, only to fall back, jostling and colliding with their neighbors and eventually entangling themselves in a welter of horns. And whenever they played like this, we knew that the grazing had been good.

Then the baby goats would be let out, so the nursing could begin. The kids would go running up to their mothers, who would assume an expression of foolish vigilance, not wishing to confuse their own offspring with someone else's—which they nonetheless did. But it was all the same to the kids—they would greedily attach themselves to the first udder that came along. Only after several eager tugs at the nipple would the mother recognize her own offspring and then either push the hungry mouth away or grow calm and contented, as if the pain caused by her own offspring were somehow different from that caused by someone else's.

As the years went by, there came to be fewer and fewer of these goats—and fewer cows too. We even began feeling a shortage of milk at home—of that same milk which, according to my grandfather, had been so plentiful in past summers that they had not had time to process it. And now this milk was all gone, and no one knew where it had disappeared to.

I remember our attic and the handwoven rug on the attic wall. Embroidered on the rug was an enormous bushy-browed deer with sad eyes and a feminine face. In the background of the rug, behind the deer, was a tiny little man. This little man stood in a hunched position and was taking aim at the deer with cruel zeal. Even as a child I could tell that this little man resented the deer and could not forgive it for being so large when he, the man, was so small. No doubt it would have been as impossible for the little man to forgive this difference in size as it would have been to change it—to make the little man large and the deer small.

And although the deer was not looking at the man, one could tell by its sad eyes that it knew exactly who he was and what he was doing. And the deer was so enormous that the man could not possibly help hitting it. The deer knew this too, but had nowhere to hide; it was so big that it could be seen from every side. In the beginning it had probably tried to flee, but now it realized that there was no escape from this hunched little man.

I would often gaze at this handwoven rug, and each time I looked at it, I was always filled with love for the deer and hatred for the hunter. And more than anything else I hated the cruel zeal of his hunched shoulders.

I miss the feel of warm muslin sheets which, after hanging all day on the porch, exude the fresh, sunny fragrance of summertime.

We children always had to go to bed before the grownups, and as we lay upstairs listening to their voices coming from the kitchen, we would also hear the voice of our own inner fears, which were somehow mysteriously bound up with the darkness of the room, the pensive creaking of the walls and, staring down from these walls, the portraits of deceased relatives, now fading away in the twilight.

And I miss even the walls of my grandfather's house, with their chestnut beams naively papered with posters, cheap reproductions, and newspaper and magazine pages. The latter dated back to the nineteen-twenties and thirties and occasionally contained some interesting items. And what fun I had reading those pages, either lying supine on the floor or standing up on a chair or couch. And sometimes, unable to restrain myself, I would tear off a particular page so that I could turn it over and read the continuation on the other side. And before long I had read each and every wall in my grandfather's house.

And what those walls did not contain!

An enormous oleograph of Napoleon abandoning the burning city of Moscow: horsemen in cocked hats, the walls of the Kremlin, and in the background a fiery glow stretching the length of the horizon.

Some pre-Revolutionary pictures on a religious theme: Christ ensconced in the clouds and wearing sandals which were laced with thongs and somehow reminiscent of our Caucasian rawhide moccasins.

Skillfully manoeuvering his prancing steed, the Archangel Gabriel slays the loathsome dragon. And right beside him, our own Soviet posters on anti-religious and agricultural themes. One of these posters I remember very well. A peasant stands at one end of a bridge which has suddenly opened up as if from some Biblical curse, and with hands thrown up in despair he watches as his horse and cart plunge downward through the gaping hole. And beneath this instructive picture appears the no less instructive caption: "If you'd thought to insure for a rainy day, at a moment like this you'd be okay!"

I never found this peasant very convincing. There was something too womanish in his reaction to the situation. The horse had barely fallen through, and yet there he was, standing idly by, throwing up his hands in despair.

Everything I had observed in real life led me to believe that no peasant would part with his horse so easily, but would do everything in his power to save it. And if, as in this case, he had lost hold of the reins, then at least he would have tried to grab hold of the horse's tail.

Once when I happened to take a long look at this peasant, I thought I detected a smile peeping out from under his mustache like some small beast of prey peering through the bushes. This smile was so unexpected that it actually startled me. I may have imagined it, of course, but if I did, I was able to do so precisely because I had always felt that there was something false about him.

The picture's caption was equally ambiguous. I could never quite figure out what was supposed to be insured—the horse or the bridge. I assumed it was the horse, but then the implication would be that the bridge should be left there to collapse, since if it were repaired, there would be no reason to insure the horse.

Perhaps the most touching and profound characteristic of childhood is an unquestioning belief in the rule of common sense. The child believes that the world is rational and hence regards everything irrational as some sort of obstacle to be pushed aside. Even when confronted by the most irrational of circumstances, the child instinctively looks for some underlying element of reason. And not doubting for a moment that it is there, he concludes that it has merely been distorted or hidden from view.

Why this belief in the rationality of things? Perhaps it is due to the fact that in childhood we still feel the throbbing of our mother's blood which once flowed through our veins and nourished us. And since the world of our mother's arms was always good to us, it is hardly surprising that we grow up believing in the goodness and rationality of this world. And how indeed could it be otherwise?

The best people, I think, are those who over the years have managed to retain this childhood faith in the world's rationality.

For it is this faith which provides man with passion and zeal in his struggle against the twin follies of cruelty and stupidity.

My grandfather's house had a reputation for hospitality and was always filled with relatives and numerous other visitors—from various and sundry officials and district Party workers on down to transient shepherds overtaken by bad weather on their annual cattle drive to summer pastures. I myself saw such visitors by the hundreds.

My uncle owned five or six cows and some fifty goats. Most of these animals were registered in the name of some relative, usually a relative from the city. The number of animals which could be owned by a single individual had for some time been restricted by law, and in our part of the country this had resulted in a sudden and mysterious blossoming of fictitious gifts, sales, and purchases.

As far as I can remember, pigs were the only animal whose numbers were not officially restricted. Knowing that the eating of pork was strictly forbidden by Islamic law, the central authorities probably assumed that the Abkhazians would not be likely to accumulate excessive numbers of pigs.

Our peasants tried as best they could to save their animals, but despite all their efforts and the use of every possible stratagem the number of livestock in our region steadily dwindled with each passing year.

And now as I thought of these animals, I suddenly remembered the period during the war when I had stayed longest at my grandfather's and for six months had had the job of tending my uncle's goats. How strange, I reflected, that so much time has passed since then—I've finished school, the Institute, and am already on my second job—and yet here I am after all these years, once again about to come face to face with these same goats who, like myself, have come up in the world and are now transforming themselves into goatibexes.

I began to recall those long-forgotten days when I was still a boy and goats were still goats and not goatibexes. And as I thought back to this period in my life, one particular evening and its adventures came suddenly to mind.

The year was 1942, and I was living at my grandfather's house in the mountains. The fear of bombings and, more important, the fear of starvation had driven me into this relatively quiet and well-nourished corner of Abkhazia.

Our home city had been bombed only twice, and probably the Germans had dropped on us the bombs that were meant for more important targets which had been too well protected for them to attack.

After the first bombing there was a mass exodus from the city. The coffeehouse orators sensibly suspended their endless political discussions and withdrew to the outlying villages where for the first time in their lives they began to appreciate the virtues of Abkhazian hominy grits.

The only people to remain in the city were those whose services were indispensable or who had nowhere to go. Since our family didn't fit into either of these categories, we soon left town along with everyone else.

After prior consultation and deliberation our country relatives parceled us out among them, taking into account our individual needs and capacities.

As a confirmed urbanite my older brother wanted to stay with the relatives whose village lay closest to the city. He got his wish, but from there was soon drafted into the army.

My sister was sent to the family of a distant relative who for some reason or other—undoubtedly his wealth—had always been considered very close to us. As the smallest and least useful member of the family I was sent off to my uncle in the mountains. Mama stayed somewhere midway between us, at the house of her older sister.

At this time my uncle still owned some twenty goats and three sheep, and no sooner had I arrived and begun to get my bearings than I found myself their newly appointed keeper.

Slowly but surely I managed to gain control over this small, obstreperous herd. What united us was the hypnotic power of two age-old expressions: "Heyt!" and "Iyoh!" These words had numerous shades of meaning, depending on how one pronounced them. The goats understood these meanings very well, but sometimes when it was to their advantage, they would confuse them.

The variety of meanings was indeed impressive. For example, if one called out "Heyt! Heyt!" loud and clear, this meant: Graze on to your heart's content, there's nothing to be afraid of.

These same sounds could be pronounced in a pedantic and reproachful tone, in which case they meant: You can't fool me, I can see where you're off to—or something to this effect. If, on the other hand, one called out "Iyoh! Iyoh!" quickly and abruptly, this was to be interpreted: Danger! Come back!

At the sound of my voice the goats would generally look up, as if trying to figure out just what it was I expected of them this time.

They always grazed with a certain disdainful look on their faces, and at times I could not help being annoyed at the way in which they would carelessly discard one half-chewed branch, only to move greedily on to another. They were capricious and wasteful, whereas we humans had to hoard every crumb. It hardly seemed fair.

Tearing the leaves from the bushes, they would rise up on their hind legs and try to get at the youngest and tenderest leaves, which were usually the farthest from reach. At such moments there was something shamelessly impudent about them, perhaps because now, raised up on their hind legs, they resembled human beings. Much later when I saw depictions of satyrs (probably in the paintings of El Greco), it occurred to me that the artist was using these weird figures to convey the very essence of human shamelessness.

The goats loved to graze on steep, precipitous slopes in close proximity to a mountain stream. I'm convinced that the sound of water whetted their appetites, just as it does our own. And in this regard it would seem no accident that when traveling in the country, we humans usually stop to eat next to a brook or stream. Apart from our need for something to drink, the very sound of running water undoubtedly makes our food seem more succulent and tasty.

The sheep usually brought up the rear and would graze with their heads bent low, as if sniffing the grass. They preferred the open and flatter areas, where I had an easy time keeping an eye on them. If something happened to frighten them, however, they would run off so quickly that it would be impossible to stop them. Their stubby tails would smack against their buttocks as they ran, and this only frightened them all the more. Thus they would continue running at breakneck speed, urged on by each successive wave of fear and agitation. And when they could run no longer, they would finally take refuge in the nearest bushes. Here they would rest for a while, heaving and panting with their mouths thrown open in doglike fashion.

The goats chose to rest in the rockiest and most elevated spots and would lie down wherever they could find a clean and uncluttered piece of ground. The highest spot would generally be occupied by the oldest male, who had terrifying horns and was hoary with age—his yellowed hair hanging in tufts along his sides. One could see that he knew his role in life: he always moved slowly, his long astrologer's beard swaying with an air of self-importance. And if in a moment of forgetfulness one of the younger males happened to usurp his place, he would calmly approach the young upstart and, without even deigning to look at him, push him away with a sidelong thrust of his horns.

Once a goat happened to disappear from the herd. I wore myself out, running from bush to bush, tearing my clothes on the thorns, and crying myself hoarse. And all to no avail; the goat was nowhere to be found. Later on, as we were returning home, I just happened to look up, and there she was—perched on the thick branch of a wild persimmon tree. Somehow she had managed to clamber up its crooked trunk. Our eyes met and she stared straight at me, but with no sign of recognition. Obviously she had no intention of getting down. I finally pelted her with a stone, and only then did she gracefully jump down and go running up to the herd.

I think goats are the most cunning of all four-legged creatures. I had only to let my mind wander a moment and sometimes they would vanish without a trace, as if swallowed up by the white stones, ferns, and walnut thickets. And how hot and frightened I would become as I ran off in pursuit of them. Lizards would dart like tiny flashes of greening lightning across the narrow, crackling path, and sometimes even a snake would appear at my feet. I would take off like a shot, and all along the bottom of the foot which had just missed stepping on the snake, I would feel the awful sensation of its cold, resilient body. I would keep on running for a long time, my legs still tingling with the giddy and almost exhilarating sensation of fear.

45

And when I could run no longer, how strange it was to stop and listen to the murmur of the bushes, wondering if perhaps this was where they had hidden; how strange to listen to the rustling of the grasshoppers, to the singing of the larks in the distant, mighty blue, or to the voice of a chance wayfarer passing along the country road which was hidden from view. And how strange to listen to the slow, strong beat of my heart as I breathed in the pungent odor of vegetation wilted by the sun. Oh, the sweet languor of a still summer day!

In good weather I would lie on the grass in the shade of a large alder tree, listening to the familiar drone of our small training planes as they flew over the mountains to where the fighting was going on.

Once as I was tending my uncle's herd, one of these planes came flying over the nearest ridge with a panic-stricken roar. It plummeted like a stone into the depths of the Kodor Valley and only at the very last minute managed to right itself. Then, without gaining any altitude it continued onward to the coast. Through every nerve of my body I could feel the almost human terror with which it had crossed over the ridge, apparently in a desperate attempt to save itself from a German fighter-bomber. With uncanny speed its shadow had skimmed across the meadow right past me, grazed a tobacco plantation and then, seconds later, could be seen passing far below along the Kodor Delta.

Every once in a while a German plane would fly over at a very high altitude. It could be recognized by its elusive wail which had something in common with the whining of a malarial mosquito. Usually when an enemy plane approached the city, our antiaircraft guns would begin to open fire, and all around it shells would explode in flowerlike clusters. But the plane would pass through them, one and all, as if protected by some magic spell. In fact, not once during the entire course of the war did I ever see one of these planes put out of action.

One of my relatives who had gone to the city to sell some pigs once arrived back with the news that my brother had been wounded. He was lying in a hospital in Baku and apparently could hardly wait for Mama's arrival. We were all very upset by the news and felt that we must get in touch with Mama as quickly as possible. Since it turned out that I was the only one who could be spared for the trip, I immediately began to make ready.

After the women had filled me up on cheese and hominy grits and Grandfather had provided me with one of his walking sticks, I finally set off, though by now it was already late in the day and the sun was hanging low in the sky, no higher than the treetops. I had all but forgotten the way, or, rather, the exact location of Uncle Meksut's house where my mother was staying, but I refused to listen to any directions. I was afraid they might change their minds about letting me go.

As best I could remember, I had first to walk through the forest which ran along the crest of the mountain and then to take the loggers' road which led down from the mountain and eventually reached Uncle Meksut's village.

Upon entering the forest, I felt as if I had suddenly plunged into a mountain stream. The warm summer day was left behind, and I made my way quickly along the path, breathing in the clean, damp coolness of the forest and listening to the vaguely disquieting rustle of the treetops. And the deeper I penetrated into the woods, the more briskly and energetically I would tap my walking stick against the firmly resilient, root-covered earth.

Out of the corner of my eye I was able to take in the beauty of my surroundings: the charming and unexpected glades covered with bright, downy grass; the silver-gray beeches with their mighty trunks; and the thick chestnut trees whose bases were heaped with last year's reddish-brown leaves. How I would have like to lie down on these leaves and rest my head on the tree's huge, moss-covered roots! In the clearings between the trees I would occasionally catch sight of the smoky-green valley and beyond it the sea, suspended between earth and sky like a mirage. Night was beginning to fall.

Suddenly from around a bend in the path there appeared two young girls. They seemed both frightened and pleased to see me. I recognized them as being from the same village, though in this setting there was something strange and unfamiliar about them—something shy and fawnlike. Their heads were lowered and they spoke in hushed, almost apologetic tones. One of them had been carrying her shoes in a bag and now was obviously embarrassed by her bare feet. She stood there scratching one foot with the other, as if trying to conceal at least one of them.

Gradually the girls' embarrassment communicated itself to me. Unable to think of anything to talk about, I quickly said good-bye. They nodded in farewell and continued quietly, even stealth-ily, on their way.

Soon afterwards I caught sight of the reddish-yellow road which led to Uncle Meksut's village. The road lay before me through the darkening trees and from a distance looked like a mountain stream. Happy at the thought of being able to walk on level ground, I quickly started down from the ridge, using my walking stick as a partial brake to avoid crashing into the dusky rhododendron bushes.

I almost fell onto the road. Yet despite the fact that my legs were covered with sweat and trembling from the strain, I imme-diately felt exhilarated by the smell of gasoline and of road dust, warm and stagnant at the end of the day. Here once again was that peculiarly city smell which had always excited me and now made me suddenly aware of how homesick I was. And although from here it was even farther to the city than from my grandfather's vil-lage, I nonetheless began to imagine that this country road would take me straight into town.

I walked along in the twilight, taking note of the tire tracks beneath my feet and rejoicing whenever I came upon a particu-larly distinct ribbed pattern. As I continued on my way, the road gradually became lighter, thanks to the enormous amber moon which was beginning to climb out from behind a jagged strip of forest.

During my summers up in the mountains I had spent many an evening gazing at the moon. It was supposed to be inhabited by a shepherd with a herd of white goats, but hard as I tried, I was never able to make out either the shepherd or his herd. Apparently one had to have seen them from earliest childhood. But all I saw when I gazed up at the moon's cold disk were some jagged, rock-hewn mountains. These mountains always made me feel sad, perhaps because they were so terribly far away and at the same time so similar to our own mountains here on earth.

Right now the moon resembled a round of smoked moun-tain cheese. With what pleasure I would have nibbled away at a hunk of this cheese, savoring its sharp taste and smoky aroma! And how I would have loved some hot grits along with it!

I hastened my steps. A sparse alder grove ran along both sides of the road, giving way in some places to corn and tobacco fields. The evening was very still; only the tapping of my stick broke the silence. Soon farmhouses began to appear, and I was cheered by their tiny, well-kept yards and by the warm, cozy glow of the fires which could be seen flickering through their half-open kitchen doors.

I listened eagerly to the sound of human voices coming from inside—sometimes faint and muffled, at other times surprisingly distinct.

"Let the dog out," I heard a male voice.

The kitchen door burst open and a dog suddenly started barking in my direction. I hastened my steps and, looking back, noticed the dark figure of a girl silhouetted in the reddish square of the open door. She stood there motionless, peering into the darkness.

Not wanting to run into any dogs, I made my way past each house as stealthily as possible. Finally I came to a wide clearing, in the middle of which stood a large walnut tree encircled with wooden benches. This was a busy spot during the day, when the villagers would gather around the kolkhoz office and store. But now, in the moonlight, the place seemed empty and forlorn, even frightening.

I remembered that somewhere near the village soviet I needed to turn left from the road onto a path. But when I reached the spot, there turned out to be several paths and I couldn't for the life of me recall which was the right one.

I stopped before one path which led off into a wild hazel grove, but couldn't decide whether to take it. I didn't remember there being any hazel bushes, but perhaps there had been after all. At one moment I would seem to recognize the path by a number of small details: its curve, the ditch that separated it from the road, and the hazel bushes. But then, the next moment it would seem that the ditch and the hazel bushes were not the same and the path itself would appear totally alien and unfamiliar.

As I stood there shifting form one foot to the other and listening to the chirring of the cicadas, my gaze wandered from the charmed stillness of the bushes up to the moon, which by now had risen high in the sky and shone with an almost blinding light, like that of a mirror.

Suddenly something black and glossy skidded onto the path and came running toward me. Before I had a chance to move, a large and powerful dog had thrust its moist nose between my legs and was sniffing me over unceremoniously. Seconds later a man appeared with a hatchet slung over his shoulder. He drove off the dog with such dispatch that I could understand why the animal had been in such a hurry to sniff me. The dog jumped away, then circled and yelped for a while, obviously eager to please its master. Finally it came to a halt by the hazel bushes and began sniffing the tracks of some animal.

The man had a bridle strapped around his middle and was apparently searching for his horse. He walked up to me and looked me over, obviously surprised to see an unfamiliar face.

"Who do you belong to, and what are you doing here?" he asked, quite annoyed at not being able to recognize me. I told him that I was trying to find Uncle Meksut's house.

"What do you need to see him for?" he asked, now in a tone of happy astonishment. Realizing that it would be hard to get the better of his peasant curiosity, I decided to tell him everything.

Glancing sideways at the dog and trying not to let it out of my sight, I began filling him in on the details, while he for his part kept shaking his head and clicking his tongue. Apparently he felt sorry that a young boy like me had to be involved in such adult matters.

"Well, Meksut lives right near here," he said, pointing down the path with his hatchet.

He began telling me the way, continually interrupting himself to express his joyful astonishment at how close Meksut's house was and how easy it was to get to. The only thing I understood from all this was that I had to follow the path. I decided not to question him any further, however, since I was already more than grateful for our encounter and for the knowledge that Meksut's house was close by.

The man now summoned his dog. I could hear the sound of its breathing as it approached, and seconds later its mighty body leapt forth from behind the bushes. The dog went running up to its master, then dropped back on its haunches and began beating the grass with its tail. Once again reminded of my existence, it gave me another quick sniff, but this time with the perfunctoriness of an official checking an I.D. card which he knows to be in order.

"It's within shouting distance—just a stone's throw away," said the man as he started off. He seemed to be thinking out loud and rejoicing at my good fortune.

The dog rushed ahead, the man's footsteps faded away, and I remained alone in the darkness.

I made my way along the path, which was overrun with hazel and blackberry bushes. In some places the bushes had locked together above the path, and I had to separate them with my stick. I passed through them as quickly as possible, but even so, the branches sometimes lashed at me from behind and I would shiver from their cold, tingling dampness. I walked along like this for some time until gradually the bushes began to thin out and all of a sudden it grew much lighter. Several minutes later I came onto a clearing and there, stretched out before me, was a cemetery gleaming brightly under the full white moon.

In my fright I recalled that I had once walked past this cemetery, but then it had been broad daylight and I had thought nothing of it. I had even knocked down several apples from a tree. And now as I spied this same tree off to one side, I tried my best to return to the carefree mood of that earlier summer day. But in vain! The tree looked completely different, hulking in the moonlight with its dark-blue foliage and pale-blue apples. I quickly stole past it.

The cemetery resembled a city of dwarfs. Its wrought-iron fencing, the green mounds of its graves, its small benches, and its tiny palaces with their wooden and metal roofs—everything in it was of miniscule proportions. Perhaps the cemetery's inhabitants had themselves grown smaller after death and now, more furtive and malevolent because of their diminished size, they continued to live out their quiet, sinister lives right here.

I noticed several small stools on which food and wine had been placed. On one of the stools there was even a candle burning inside a glass jar. I had heard of the custom of offering up food and drink to the dead, but nonetheless the sight of these stools frightened me all the more.

The crickets continued their chirring and the moon cast its white light on the already white gravestones, making their black shadows look even blacker as they lay on the earth, heavy and immobile like slabs of rock.

I stole past the graves as quietly as I could, but my stick made a hollow and slightly terrifying sound as it tapped against the ground. I drew it up under my arm, but now the night became so still that I was even more frightened. Suddenly I noticed a coffin lid leaning against the wrought-iron fence enclosing one of the graves. Next to this grave was a new, freshly dug plot which had not yet been fenced in.

At the sight of the coffin lid a quiver of icy cold shot up my spine, painfully contracted the skin on the back of my neck, and actually made my hair stand on end. But I kept on walking—my eyes fastened on the coffin lid, which cast a reddish glow in the moonlight.

According to Islamic custom the coffin of the deceased is lowered into the grave without any lid, apparently to facilitate the dead man's ascent to heaven. Once inside the grave, the coffin is covered over with loose boards which perform the same function as a lid.

But I knew nothing of this custom at the time and assumed in my ignorance that the dead man had come out of his grave, rested his coffin lid against the fence, and was now wandering around somewhere in the vicinity. Or perhaps he was hiding behind the lid, just waiting for me to turn my back on him and start running. But I continued to walk, not moving one extra muscle and not accelerating my steps, knowing that I must keep my eyes on the coffin lid, no matter what. At the sound of grass rustling beneath my feet, I realized that I had strayed from the path, but I kept on walking, not letting the lid out of sight. Suddenly I felt myself falling.

I caught a momentary glimpse of the moon streaking across the sky and then plopped onto something white and hairy which immediately shot out from under me. I fell back onto the ground, apparently at the bottom of a large pit. As I lay there with closed eyes, awaiting my fate, I sensed that he, or rather *it*, was somewhere beside me and that I was completely in its power. And now there began flashing through my mind scenes from stories I had heard shepherds and hunters tell of graveyard happenings and strange encounters in the forest.

I lay there terror-stricken and utterly helpless, but for some reason the apparition made no move in my direction. Finally, when I could stand the suspense no longer, I summoned up the courage to open my eyes.

It was as if I had flung open a door into a pitch-black room. At first I couldn't see a thing, but then I noticed something whitish moving in the darkness. I could feel that it was watching me, but more frightening than this was its strange swaying motion.

I have no idea how many minutes went by, but gradually I began to regain the use of my senses. First I recognized the smell of freshly dug earth still warm from the heat of the day; then I detected some other, very familiar and almost reassuring smell which somehow reminded me of home. Still swaying and white, the apparition remained in its corner, but my horror, which had seemed to last an eternity, had finally spent itself. I now became aware of a pain in my leg and felt a need to stretch it out full length. I had apparently sprained it during my fall.

For a long time I kept my eyes fastened on the wavering white spot. Suddenly it began to take on a familiar shape, and seconds later it turned into a male goat with horns and a beard which were clearly discernible even in the darkness. Having long known that the devil often assumes the form of a goat, I felt somewhat reassured, since at least this much was clear. One thing I hadn't realized, however, was that the devil would also smell like a goat.

I cautiously extended my leg, but this seemed to put the goat on his guard. He stopped chewing his cud and merely continued to sway back and forth in his strange fashion.

I immediately froze in position and once again the goat went back to his cud. Summoning up my courage, I raised my head and now was able to see the edge of the pit, sharply etched in the moonlight, and a translucent strip of sky, in the middle of which gleamed a small bright star. A tree rustled in the distance, and it was strange to be able to sense from down here the breeze that was blowing up there. I looked up at the tiny star and noticed that it too seemed to sway slightly in the breeze. Suddenly there was a hollow thud. An apple had fallen from the apple tree. I gave a start, now realizing for the first time that it was growing chilly.

Some boyish instinct told me that inaction is never a sign of strength. And since the goat continued to chew, gazing right

53

through me as if I didn't exist, I decided I would try to escape. I stood up cautiously and extended my arm, only to discover that the edge was too high for me to reach even by jumping. My walking stick had remained up above, but probably it wouldn't have helped me much anyway.

The pit was quite narrow, and I decided I would try to scale it at an angle, pressing my arms against one wall and my legs against the other. Groaning from the strain, I managed to raise myself a few short feet, but then one of my legs—the bad one—slid from the wall and once again I landed on the ground. As I fell, the goat jumped up in fright and shied to one side. This was very careless of him, since now I grew bolder and even approached him. As he backed into his corner without making a sound, I cautiously extended my hand. He touched the palm of my hand with his lips and I could feel his warm breath. Then obstinately shaking his head, he began sniffing and snorting in goatlike fashion.

I was now fully convinced that this was no devil but merely a goat which had landed in the same mess as I. I had often noticed when tending my uncle's herd that goats have a habit of getting stuck in spots which they're unable to get out of.

I sat down on the ground next to the goat, putting my arms around his neck and pressing close to his body. I tried to make him lie down so that I could get the full benefit of his warmth, but he stubbornly continued to stand. He did, however, begin to lick my hand—cautiously at first, then ever more boldly. His strong, supple tongue ran roughly along my palm, licking the salt from it. I enjoyed the prickly sensation and did not remove my hand. The goat was enjoying himself too and had already begun to fasten his sharp teeth on the edge of my shirt. I quickly rolled up my shirt sleeve and let him move on to fresh territory.

As he continued licking my arm, I realized for the first time in my life how comforting the presence of another living creature can be. It now occurred to me that even if the ashen blue face of the dead man were suddenly to peer over the top of the pit, I would not be too frightened but would merely press closer to my goat.

After a while the goat grew tired of licking my arm and lay down beside me of his own accord. Here he remained, peacefully chewing his cud.

The night was as still as ever, only the moonlight had grown more limpid and the tiny star had moved to the edge of the strip of sky. It had also grown chillier.

Suddenly I heard the sound of approaching hoofbeats, and my heart began pounding madly. The hoofbeats became more and more distinct, and at times I could even hear the metallic clicking of the horse's shoes against the stones. I was afraid the rider would turn off to the side, but the hoofbeats kept coming closer and closer and already I could hear the horse's breathing and the squeaking of the saddle. I was too excited to move, and only when the hoofbeats had passed almost directly overhead did I finally jump up and start shouting, "Help! Help! I'm down here!"

The horse came quickly to a halt and in the silence I could distinguish the bonelike crunching of its teeth against the bit. Then a male voice asked hesitantly, "Who's there?"

I lurched forward in the direction of the voice and cried out, "It's me! A boy!"

The man was silent for a moment and then I heard, "What boy?"

The man's voice was hard and suspicious. Apparently he feared some sort of trap.

"I'm a boy from the city," I said, trying to sound as much like a living person as possible, which only made my voice sound strange and unnatural.

"What are you doing down there?" the voice asked gruffly. The man still suspected a trap.

"I fell in by accident, I was on my way to Uncle Meksut's," I quickly replied, afraid that he would ride on before I could finish.

"To Meksut's? You should have said so."

I heard him get down from his horse and throw the reins over the wrought-iron fence of one of the graves. His footsteps drew nearer, but then he suddenly halted before reaching the edge of the pit.

"Grab hold," he shouted as a rope came whirring down through the air and landed in the pit beside me. As I grabbed hold of it, I suddenly remembered the goat, which was standing silent and forlorn in his corner. After a moment's reflection I wound the rope around his neck in a double loop and cried up:

"You can start pulling!"

As the rope grew taut, the goat began jerking his head and rising up on his hind legs. In order to prevent the rope from biting into his neck, I grabbed hold of his hind legs and began pushing up with all my strength. But just as his horned head appeared in the moonlight above the pit, the man suddenly let out a howl in what seemed a goatlike voice, dropped the rope and took to his heels. The goat came crashing down beside me and I cried out in pain as one of his hoofs landed on my foot. My tears must have been close to the surface since now I began crying in earnest—from weariness and frustration as well as from the pain. I kept on crying till I could cry no longer. But then, just as I was cursing myself for not having warned the man about the goat, it suddenly occurred to me that the man's horse was still tied to the fence and that eventually he would have to come back for it.

And sure enough, about ten minutes later I caught the sound of footsteps creeping up in the distance. Obviously he intended to untie his horse and take off as quickly as possible.

"That was a goat," I said in a loud but calm voice.

Silence.

"Mister, that was a goat," I repeated, trying to maintain the same tone of voice.

I sensed that he had halted and was listening.

"Whose goat?" he asked suspiciously.

"I don't know, he fell in before I did," I answered, realizing that my words did not sound very convincing.

"You don't seem to know anything, do you?" he remarked. "And how are you related to Meksut?"

Too excited to make any sense, I began explaining our relationship (in Abkhazia everyone is related). I felt he was beginning to believe me, and hoping to inspire his confidence even further, I went on to explain the purpose of my visit. But the more I talked, the more I realized how difficult it is to justify oneself from the depths of the grave.

Finally he made his way up to the pit and cautiously leaned forward. His unshaven face looked strange and unsavory in the moonlight, and it was obvious that he would rather have been anywhere but here at the edge of this pit. I even had the impression that he was holding his breath.

56

I threw up the end of the rope which had fallen back into the pit and tried to help him from below as he grabbed hold and began pulling. The goat foolishly resisted, but after hoisting him up halfway, the man managed to seize hold of his horns and with ill-concealed aversion hauled him out of the pit. He was obviously disgusted by the whole business.

"Goddamned beast!" he muttered, and I heard the sound of his foot kicking the goat. The goat bleated in pain and must have darted off, for now the man began swearing in earnest. But apparently he seized hold of the rope in time, and seconds later I heard the goat being dragged back again. Now the man knelt down by the edge of the pit and, planting one hand on the ground, seized my outstretched hand with the other and angrily began pulling. I tried to make myself as light as possible, not wanting to get the same treatment as the goat. He quickly hoisted me up over the edge of the pit and set me down beside him. He was a large, heavy-set man, and my hand ached from his grip.

After looking me over in silence, he suddenly flashed a smile and patted me on the head, "You gave me quite a scare with that goat of yours. There I was, thinking there was a human at the other end of the rope, and out comes that horned creature..."

I immediately felt better. We walked over to the fence where his horse stood motionless and clearly visible in the moonlight. The goat trailed behind us, still tied to the rope.

From the horse came the sweet smell of sweat, saddle leather and corn. Probably he's just left some corn off at the mill, I thought, remembering that the rope too had smelled of corn. The man now lifted, or rather threw, me into the saddle, whereupon the horse tossed back its head and tried to bite me. I drew up my leg just in time. Suddenly I remembered my walking stick, but didn't dare ask permission to go back for it.

The man loosened the reins from the fence, tossed them over the horse's head and climbed heavily into the saddle—all the while holding the goat by his tether. The horse sagged under his weight and I myself was squeezed uncomfortably between his body and the saddlebow.

The horse set off briskly, kicking up its heels and trying to break into a trot. It was full of energy and obviously resented having to drag the goat along behind it.

Lulled by the dull reverberation of the horse's hoofbeats and by its gentle, rocking gait, I dozed off.

Suddenly the horse came to a halt and I awoke. We were standing by a wattle fence behind which could be seen a well-tended yard and a large house set high on wooden pilings. A light was burning in the window. It was Uncle Meksut's house.

"Hey! Where's the master of the house?" shouted my companion as he lit up a cigarette. Not bothering to get down from the saddle, he carelessly slung the goat's tether around one of the fence pickets.

The door of the house opened and someone called out, "Who's there?"

The voice was bold and sharp and seemed to indicate a readiness for any encounter. Such is the tone of voice in which people in our parts respond to an unfamiliar cry at night.

It was Uncle Meksut. I immediately recognized his short, broad-shouldered figure. He came down the steps and started toward us, peering intently into the darkness and chasing off the dogs which crowded around him.

I can still remember the astonished and even frightened look on his face when he finally caught sight of me.

"It's a long story," said my rescuer, lifting me out of the saddle and trying to pass me over the fence into Uncle Meksut's arms. But I refused to be passed, and catching hold of one of the pickets, I climbed down on my own. My companion began to unwind the goat's tether from the fence.

"Where did the goat come from?" asked Uncle Meksut, now even more astonished.

"It's quite a story, quite a story!" the horseman gaily replied, casting a conspiratorial glance in my direction.

"Leave your horse and come on inside!" said Uncle Meksut, grabbing the horse by the bit.

"Thanks, Meksut, but I'm afraid I can't," answered the horseman, suddenly preparing to leave, though up to now he hadn't seemed in any hurry. As dictated by Abkhazian custom, Uncle Meksut tried long and hard to persuade him to stay—first acting offended, then pleading, and finally even making fun of the alleged obligations which prevented him from accepting his hospitality. As he talked, Uncle Meksut kept glancing back and forth between me and the goat, apparently sensing that the goat

58

was somehow connected with my arrival, but just how, he could not for the life of him figure out.

Finally the horseman rode off, dragging the goat behind him. Uncle Meksut led me into the house, clicking his tongue in astonishment and scolding the dogs as he went.

The front room was filled with guests. They were seated around a large table covered with fruit and refreshments, and their faces were clearly illuminated—more by the flaming hearth than by the light given off by the kerosene lamp. Mama was there too, and even in the crimson glow of the flames I could see the color slowly drain from her face as she caught sight of me.

The other guests jumped up from their seats, gasping and groaning in astonishment. Upon learning the purpose of my visit, one of my city aunts began to topple backward as if in a faint. Having little experience in such matters, none of her country relatives came to the rescue and she was forced to catch herself awkwardly in midfall.

Uncle Meksut did his best to comfort the women and even proposed a toast to victory, to our sons and to the safe return of all of them. Uncle Meksut was the soul of hospitality; his house was always filled with guests, and now that the grapes had already been harvested here in the valley, the season of lengthy toasts was just beginning.

Mama sat quietly, not touching a thing. I felt sorry for her and would have liked to comfort her, but the role I had chosen for myself did not permit any such display of weakness.

A bowl of steaming grits, some roast chicken and even a glass of wine were set before me now. Mama shook her head disapprovingly at the wine, but Uncle Meksut said that *macharka* was as harmless as grape juice and that I was no longer a child.

I had finished relating my adventures and was still sucking the meat from the last of the chicken bones when suddenly I felt sleep coming over me—a sleep as sweet and golden as *macharka*, the first wine of the season. I dozed off at the table.

Mama returned from Baku some ten days later. It turned out that my brother had not been wounded at all, but was merely homesick. He had decided that he had to see at least one member of the family before being sent off to the front and, as usual, he got his way. He was the prankster in our family and such a stunt was completely in character.

IV

It was about ten in the morning and already beginning to get hot when I arrived in the village of Walnut Springs. The bus let me off and continued on its way, leaving a trail of dust behind it.

I began walking in the direction of the kolkhoz office, only too happy to be able to stretch my legs after the long bus ride. I was in a good mood and fairly brimming with reportorial zeal.

Next to the kolkhoz office I noticed two elderly Abkhazians seated in a patriarchal pose under the mighty canopy of a walnut tree. One of them held a staff in his hand, the other a walking stick. I was surprised and delighted to observe that the hooklike curve at the top of the staff exactly matched the hooklike contour of its owner's nose, while the straight and simple line of the walking stick held by the second old man was equally in keeping with his straight, Roman nose. I nodded to the old men in passing and they politely bent forward, as if half rising to greet me.

"That's the new doctor, I expect," said one of them after I had passed by.

"He looks more like an Armenian to me," said the other.

The kolkhoz administration was housed in a two-story wooden building. The offices were on the second floor, while the first floor was given over to the kolkhoz store and to various storerooms whose doors were bolted with heavy padlocks. The door to the store was open, and from inside came the sound of female laughter.

An old battered car was parked out front, and I gathered that the kolkhoz chairman was in his office.

Tacked to the front wall of the building was an announcement written in ink-stained letters which read as follows:

THE GOATIBEX IS OUR PRIDE AND JOY

A lecture to be given by Vakhtang Bochua, doctoral candidate in archeology, active member of the Society for the Advancement of Scientific and Political Knowledge, and chairman of the Society for the Preservation of the Treasures of Antiquity.

The lecture will be followed by a showing of the film *The Iron Mask*.

So Vakhtang was already here or about to arrive! I was delighted at the thought of a reunion with our renowned joker and *changalist*. I hadn't seen Vakhtang in more than a year, and although I had heard he was doing well, I had no idea that he had already become a doctoral candidate in archeology, much less an authority on goatibexes.

Here I should explain that the word *changalist*, which seems to be used only in Abkhazia, signifies a person who likes to drink at others' expense. The verb *zachangalit'*, derived from this word, means to latch onto someone and take control, not necessarily for the purpose of a free drink, but sometimes in a broader sense.

Actually, most of us didn't mind treating Vakhtang, since wherever he went he always created a mood of noisy, unrestrained gaiety. Even his appearance was full of comic contradictions: he was a native of the Caucasus, but as fair as the fairest Swede; he had the gloomy and massive head of a Nero, but was good-natured and gentle; he could be as pushy and resourceful as any State procurement agent, but was a historian and curator by profession.

Following his graduation from the Institute of Historical and Archival studies, Vakhtang had worked for several years as a tour guide. Then he had published a short book entitled *Among the Flowering Ruins* which had become a favorite with our tourists. "And with foreign tourists," Vakhtang would inevitably add whenever the subject came up in his presence, which it almost always did since he himself was sure to bring it up.

We Abkhazians had often gotten together during our student days in Moscow, and there was never a party that took place

61

without Vakhtang. In this respect, as in many others, he showed an extraordinary sense of timing. If, for example, one of us happened to receive a package from home, Vakhtang never had to be informed of the fact but would automatically appear in the dormitory of the student in question before the latter even had a chance to open his package.

"Stop the proceedings," he would shout from the hall. Then as he came bursting into the room, he would overwhelm the unfortunate recipient with a torrent of eloquent but meaningless words.

One sensed the operator in him even then, but he was a gay, impudent and artistic sort of operator—and really quite harmless and good-natured except on those rare occasions when he personally had to foot the bill.

With my mind on Vakhtang I made my way up the wooden stairs and entered the kolkhoz office, which consisted of a single long, cool room partitioned in half by two wooden railings. To my left, a stout, unshaven individual sat dozing at his desk. Sensing that someone had entered, he half opened one eye and briefly took cognizance of my arrival. Then, his curiosity satisfied, he dozed off again. He was like a sleepy tomcat which half opens one eye at the sound of dishes clattering in the distance, only to close it once he realizes that this clatter has nothing to do with the beginning of a meal.

To my right, several accountants were industriously clicking away on their abacuses. Occasionally, when one of them would click too loudly, the dozing individual would half open the same eye and then amiably close it again. One of the accountants got up from his desk, walked over to the metal cabinet and took a folder from it. Only as he turned away from the cabinet did I suddenly realize that this accountant was a girl dressed in a man's suit. I was struck by the expression on her face; it was as sad as a dried-up well.

At the far end of the room the imposing figure of the chairman loomed from behind a large desk. He was talking on the telephone. He looked me over with cool curiosity and then averted his eyes, apparently intent upon what was being said at the other end of the receiver.

"Hello," I said in Russian, not addressing anyone in particular.

"Hello," the girl answered softly, slightly raising her sad face.

I didn't know what to say or do next. It would have been embarrassing to interrupt the chairman while he was still on the phone, but it was equally embarrassing just to stand there doing nothing.

"Has the lecturer arrived yet?" I asked the girl on the spur of the moment, as if it were the lecture I was interested in.

"Yes, Comrade Bochua has already arrived," she softly replied, looking up at me with her large round eyes, "but he's gone off to have a look at the old fortress."

"My dear fellow, there's no need to worry about the corn, the stalks are as sturdy as saplings!" the chairman began thundering in Abkhazian. "As sturdy as saplings, I tell you. But what I wanted to remind you about was the fertilizer.... Yes, they've sent us some, but not enough.... If that idiotic commission should come around, just bring them over. We've got plenty to show for ourselves.... May I dig up my father's bones if we don't manage to fulfill the plan, but my dear Andrey Sharlovich, as for extra land, we simply don't have any.... What fallow lands?! We haven't enough fallow lands to spread a handkerchief on. Our agronomist is sitting right here, he'll tell you—if he ever wakes up, that is," the chairman added playfully, now glancing over at the individual who was dozing.

But no sooner had he finished his sentence than the latter began gurgling something angrily in reply—before even opening his eyes, as it seemed to me. From what he said, I gathered that he had no intention of rooting up his tea plantations for any crazy commissioners. And having made his point, he broke off as precipitously as he had begun, closing his eyes in midsentence.

The chairman kept his hand cupped firmly over the receiver while the agronomist was talking. But now as he noticed that I was watching him, he frowned and barked out in Abkhazian to the girl:

"Find out where that blockhead is from and what he wants!"

Returning once again to the receiver, he suddenly adopted the tone of a mildly reproachful host:

"You've been neglecting us, Andrey Sharlovich. It doesn't seem right. And it's not just me who's asking for you, but the people—our kolkhoz workers."

I was somewhat taken aback by the word blockhead. Since the chairman had obviously concluded that I wasn't a native Abkhazian, I had no choice but to play along.

The chairman was still talking on the telephone. By now he had come full circle and was back on the subject of fertilizer:

"About a hundred tons of superphosphate. Please, Andrey Sharlovich, I beseech you as a brother."

I watched the girl as she worked. She was adding up something and every once in a while she would move the counters of her abacus as if pensively toying with a strand of large wooden beads.

Finally the chairman hung up the receiver and I walked up to him.

"Hello, comrade. You're from the State lumber yards, right?" he asked confidently as he extended his hand.

"I'm from the newspaper," I answered.

"Welcome," he said, growing more alert and apparently shaking my hand somewhat harder than he had intended.

"Here are my credentials," I said, reaching into my pocket.

"Oh, that won't be necessary," he replied with a peremptory wave of the hand. "One can always tell an honest man by his face," he had the impudence to add, looking me straight in the eye.

"I'm here in connection with the goatibex," I said, immediately sensing that anything I had to say on the subject would only sound ludicrous in this company. And I was right. One of the accountants began to chuckle.

"Cut the laughter, you hear!" muttered the chairman in Abkhazian and then added in Russian: "We've made great strides with the goatibex."

"And what specifically?" I asked.

"Well, in the first place we've launched a full-scale campaign to educate the people," said the chairman, bending back the little finger of his left hand and tapping it against his right palm for emphasis. "Today, for example, our respected colleague Vakhtang Bochua is giving a lecture on the goatibex. And we've sent our livestock man off to consult with the breeding specialist," he added, now bending back his fourth finger and again tapping it lightly against his palm. "Why—are there any complaints?" he asked, suddenly stopping short and gazing at me with dark, wary eyes.

"No," I answered, meeting his gaze head-on.

"Well, there's this one individual, the former chairman of a kolkhoz that was merged with ours, and he...."

"No, no," I broke in, "this has nothing to do with any complaints."

"But he never signs his name," he added, as if to reveal the full extent of the man's cunning. "But we know who he is and how he signs his letters."

"Can I have a look at the goatibex?" I interrupted, letting him know that this individual didn't interest me in the least.

"Of course," he answered, "let's go."

The chairman got up from his desk, his large, powerful body moving freely and easily under his loose clothing.

Without saying a word, the sleepy agronomist rose from his desk and accompanied us down to the porch.

"How many times have I told that idiot to clean up the sheep pen," said the chairman in Abkhazian as we descended the stairs.

"Valiko! Come here a minute!" shouted the chairman, still in Abkhazian, as he turned toward the door which led into the store. "Or have they already married you off in there?"

From inside the store came the sound of a girl's laughter and a young man's impudent voice:

"What's the matter?"

"It's not what *is* the matter, but what's *going* to be the matter if I lock you two up in there and invite your mother-in-law to come see for herself what's going on!"

The sound of female laughter was heard once again, and now there appeared on the threshold a young man of medium height with enormous blue eyes which gazed with childlike innocence from his swarthy face.

"Drive over to Auntie Nutsa's and get some cucumbers for the goatibex," said the chairman. "A comrade has come from the city and we don't want to be disgraced."

"No thanks, not me," said the young man, "they'd laugh in my face."

"The hell with them—this is State business," the chairman declared sternly. "Then take the cucumbers straight to the pen—we'll be waiting for you there."

Apparently this young man Valiko was the chairman's driver. He got into the car, started it up, and with an angry turn of the wheel drove out into the street.

It had grown hot. The two old men were still sitting in the shade of the walnut tree. The one with the staff was relating something to his companion, and as he talked, he would tap the ground every so often with his staff. He had gouged a decent-sized hole already, and one could easily imagine that here in this shady spot he was planning to erect a picket fence to protect himself and his companion from the hot summer sun and the bustle of kolkhoz life.

The chairman greeted the two old men as we approached, and they went through the motions of half rising to greet us.

"Sonny," asked the one with the staff, "is that young fellow with you the new doctor?"

"He's the goatibex doctor," replied the chairman.

"And here I thought he was an Armenian," interjected the one with the stick.

"Will wonders never cease!" exclaimed the one with the staff. "Why up in the mountains I used to kill those goatibexes by the hundreds, and now they send a doctor for just one of them.

"That old man's quite a cunning fellow," remarked the chairman when we had reached the street.

"How so?" I asked.

"Well, one time when the district Party secretary was driving by, he happened to stop in this spot. That old man was sitting there in the shade, just as he is now, and the two of them start talking about how things used to be in the old days and how they are today. The old man says to him, 'They used to plough the earth with wooden ploughs, but now they use metal ones.' 'So?' asks the secretary. 'With the wooden plough the earth falls equally to both sides, but the metal plough throws it all to one side,' says the old man. 'Well, what does that prove?' asks the secretary. 'If the earth falls equally to both sides, then the peasant gets to keep only half of the harvest for himself, and the other half goes to the master. But the metal plough throws the earth all to *one* side, and that means that the peasant gets all the harvest for himself.' 'Right you are,' says the secretary and with that he drives off."

I decided to jot down this anecdote so as not to forget it later on. But no sooner had I reached for my notebook than the chairman broke in decisively:

"That's not necessary."

"Why not?" I asked in surprise.

"It's not worth it," he said, "that's just an old man's idle rambling. Don't worry, I'll tell you when there's something worth writing down."

"Well, never mind, I'll remember it anyway," I thought to myself as I put away my notebook.

We made our way along the scorched, dusty road. By now the dust had grown so hot that I could feel it baking through the soles of my shoes.

On either side of the road small farmhouses with their fruit trees, private plots of corn, and green patchwork of lawns would occasionally come into view. The trunks and branches of the fruit trees were overgrown with grapevines, and thick clusters of unripened grapes could be seen peeping through the curly foliage of the vines.

"There'll be a lot of wine this year," I remarked to the chairman.

"Yes, the grapes are good," he replied somewhat absent-mindedly, "but have you noticed the corn?"

I looked at the corn, but didn't notice anything in particular.

"Why, what's there to notice?" I asked.

"Take a good look," said the chairman, smiling enigmatically.

"Upon closer inspection I noticed that the corn on one side of each private plot was higher and had thicker and greener leaves than on the other side.

"Was it planted at different times?" I asked the chairman, who continued to smile enigmatically.

"The very same day, the very same hour," he replied, his smile growing even broader.

"What's the explanation?" I asked.

"This year there was a reduction in the size of private plots—a necessary measure, of course, but not for our kolkhoz. Tea is our main crop, so what use are these scraps of land to me? I can't use them for raising tea."

67

I took another good look at the corn. And indeed, the difference in the size and strength of the stalks was so pronounced that I was reminded of those textbook drawings used to project future crop yields.

"These peasants are very clever," said the chairman, still smiling enigmatically. And now his smile seemed to indicate that no city person had ever understood, nor was ever likely to understand, just how clever these peasants could be.

"In what way?" I asked.

"In what way? Go ahead, you tell him," said the chairman, suddenly turning to the agronomist.

"Well, for example, if a peasant sees some cow dung lying here on the road, he'll automatically throw it onto his plot—but only onto the part that still belongs to him," wheezed the agronomist. "And it's that way with everything they do."

"That's peasant psychology for you," said the chairman condescendingly.

I wanted to jot down this bit about the cow dung, but once again the chairman grabbed my arm and forced me to put away my notebook.

"What's wrong with writing it down?" I asked.

"This is just casual conversation, not the sort of thing you should write about," he replied with all the conviction of a man who knew better than I what one could and could not write about.

"But it's the truth, isn't it?" I asked in astonishment.

"But do you think every truth can be written down?" he asked, equally astonished.

And here we were both so astonished at the other's astonishment that we burst out laughing. The agronomist snorted disdainfully.

"If I should tell them," said the chairman, nodding in the direction of the nearest plot, "that they could keep half of the harvest from the whole plot, then they'd work the land quite differently and take in a good harvest from both parts."

I already knew that such things went on in many kolkhozes, though of course not too openly.

"Well, why couldn't you tell them that?" I asked.

"It would be considered a violation of the law," he sternly replied and then added somewhat vaguely, "though sometimes we do allow them to keep half of whatever's been harvested over and above the plan."

Suddenly I was struck by the heavy aroma of sun-steamed tea leaves, and seconds later the tea plantation came into view— its dark-green rows of bushes extending from the right-hand side of the road all the way up to the edge of the forest. In some places the bushes gently skirted the forest, while in others they entered it, forming a sort of cove. An enormous oak stood in the middle of the plantation, and it was undoubtedly here that the tea pickers found relief from the noonday sun.

All around us it was so still that one would have thought the plantation was deserted. But now the broad-brimmed hat of one of the pickers suddenly appeared by the side of the road, while farther away there flashed a white kerchief and then a third figure in red.

"How's it going, Gogola?" the agronomist called out to the figure in the broad-brimmed hat. The hat turned in our direction.

"Twenty kilos since morning," said the girl, briefly raising her pretty, delicate face.

"Good girl, Gogola!" the chairman shouted happily.

The agronomist wheezed with satisfaction.

The girl bent gracefully over the tea bush and began skimming its surface with an almost caressing movement of her nimble fingers. She had gloves on her hands, but they were gloves with the fingers cut out, like those worn during the winter by lady streetcar conductors in Moscow.

The only sound to break the silence was the steady plop! plop! plop! of the tender shoots which seemed to jump of their own accord into the hands of the young picker, and from there into the basket. The latter was attached to her belt and pulled it down slightly to one side. She made her way slowly along the row of bushes, moving her hands back and forth from bush to basket and every once in a while bending over to pull out a weed from one of the bushes.

By now the heat had grown intense and there was a slight haziness on the horizon.

The sight of the tea plantation and the steady, quiet work of the almost invisible pickers seemed to have a heartening effect on the chairman.

"Good girl, Gogola, good girl!" he called out, almost crooning with satisfaction.

Still breathing heavily, the agronomist strode alongside us.

"You should put something down about Gogola, I'll tell you all about her," said the chairman. "Last summer she picked eighteen hundred kilos—almost two tons."

But by now I didn't feel like putting anything down and, more to the point, this was not the story I was after.

"Another time," I answered. "Tell me, have you and the other kolkhoz been merged for long?"

"That's a sore subject, my dear fellow. They've saddled us with a bunch of losers," replied the chairman with distaste and then added: "This consolidation business—it's a good measure, of course, but not for our kolkhoz. Their crop is tobacco, ours is tea. I'd rather raise *ten* goatibexes than have anything to do with those people."

"Ah, good girl, Gogola, good girl," he crooned once again, as if hoping to restore his good mood. But apparently his efforts were in vain, for he suddenly spat out in disgust: "Losers! Real losers!"

Then he grew silent.

We finally reached the area where the animals were kept. Next to a large, empty cowshed was a pen with wattle fencing, which was used for the animals in the summertime. This pen was adjoined by a smaller one, and it was here that we found the goatibex resting under a thin canvas awning.

As we approached the pen, I eagerly began examining the illustrious animal. As soon as he caught sight of us, the goatibex stopped chewing his cud and glared with pink, unblinking eyes in our direction. Then he rose to his feet and with a forward thrust of his powerful chest began stretching himself. He was a surprisingly large animal with massive horns which curled outward like a well-cultivated Cossack mustache.

"He's healthy enough, but he's just not interested in our female goats," said the chairman.

"What do you mean, not interested?"

"He doesn't mate with any of them," explained the chairman, "our climate's too humid. He's used to the mountains."

"And you say you feed him with cucumbers?" I asked, suddenly recoiling as I remembered that he had talked about the cucumbers in Abkhazian. Fortunately, however, my slip of the tongue went unnoticed.

"What do you mean!" he exclaimed. "We give him the regular, prescribed diet. The cucumbers are just an extra—a bit of local initiative on our part."

The chairman thrust his hand into the pen and began coaxing the goatibex. The goatibex fixed his gaze on the chairman's hand, but didn't budge an inch.

At this point Valiko drove up. He got out of the car and as he started toward us—his pockets bulging with cucumbers—the agronomist sat down beside the fence and immediately dozed off in its meager shade. The chairman relieved Valiko of one of the cucumbers and extended his hand through the fence. The goatibex pricked up his ears and fastened his gaze on the cucumber. Then, as if hypnotized, he began to move slowly forward. But just when he had come within a few feet of the cucumber, the chairman lifted his hand so high that the goatibex was unable to reach it. The animal now proceeded to raise himself up on his hind legs, resting his forelegs on the fence. But no sooner had he extended his neck in the direction of the cucumber than the chairman raised his hand even higher. This was too much to bear, and now with one light, savage spring the goatibex leaped over the fence, almost landing on the agronomist's head. The latter just barely opened his eyes and then dozed off again.

"His jumping ability is quite extraordinary," solemnly declared the chairman as he surrendered the cucumber.

Baring his large yellow incisors, the goatibex seized the cucumber and began chewing on it with the frenzied impatience of a cat attacking a ball of catnip.

"You'll have to climb over and coax him back in again," said the chairman, turning to his driver.

Valiko groaned in disgust and climbed over the fence, accidentally dropping several cucumbers from his pockets. The goatibex would have pounced on them, but the chairman quickly chased him away and picked up the cucumbers himself. From inside the fence Valiko held up one of his remaining cucumbers and began coaxing the animal back into the pen. The chairman

71

offered me one of the cucumbers that had fallen on the ground and himself bit into another, first rubbing it lightly on his sleeve.

"Most of our animals are pasturing up in the mountains," said the chairman, smacking his lips as he ate. "We've kept ten of our best she-goats down here for him, but he's just not responding."

Once again the goatibex raised himself up, placing his forelegs on the fence. But still unable to reach the cucumber, he jumped back into the pen with an even more impressive leap than before. No sooner was he inside, however, than the driver raised the cucumber high above his head. The goatibex stopped dead in his tracks and fixed his pink, animal eyes on the cucumber. Then he jumped up, tore the cucumber from the driver's hand, and crashed to the ground.

"He almost bit off my fingers," grumbled Valiko as he took another cucumber from his pocket and bit into it.

All of us were now munching on cucumbers except for the agronomist, who still lay dozing against the fence.

"Hey," shouted the chairman, "maybe this will wake you up!" And he tossed him a cucumber.

The agronomist opened his eyes and picked up the cucumber. He wiped it lethargically on his linen tunic and was about to bite into it, but then for some reason changed his mind. He put the cucumber into his pocket and dozed off again.

A little boy and girl, both about eight years old, came walking up to the pen. The little girl had a large ear of corn in her arms, which she cradled like a baby. The ear must have just been picked, since there were beads of moisture on the silky hairs protruding from beneath its green husk.

"I think the goatibex is about to start a fight," said the little boy.

"We'd better go home," said the little girl.

"We'll watch him fight and then we'll go," declared the little boy.

"Try letting in the goats," said the chairman.

The driver walked over and opened the gate leading into the other pen. Only now did I notice that in a corner of this larger pen a group of she-goats lay huddled together, dozing.

"Heyt, heyt!" shouted Valiko as he began to rouse them.

The goats got up unwillingly and now, raising his head in alarm, the goatibex began sniffing in their direction.

"He understands," said the chairman, obviously delighted.

"Heyt, heyt!" Valiko kept shouting as he tried to herd the goats together and drive them through the open gate into the smaller pen. But the goats refused to go near the gate and kept running off in every direction.

"They're afraid," said the chairman joyfully.

The goatibex stood stock-still with his neck craned forward and his eyes glued on the gate. As he watched and sniffed, his upper lip would occasionally quiver, and I had the impression he was baring his teeth.

"He hates them," said the chairman almost ecstatically.

"Let's go home," said the little girl, "I'm scared."

"Don't be scared," said the little boy and then added with enthusiasm: "He's gonna start fighting right away."

"I can't help being scared. He's awful wild," the little girl said soberly as she pressed the ear of corn to her chest.

"He's stronger than all those goats put together," said the little boy.

The agronomist suddenly began to chuckle, and taking the cucumber from his pocket, he broke it in half and offered it to the two children. The little girl didn't move an inch, but merely hugged the ear of corn all the more tightly to her chest. After a moment's hesitation the little boy edged forward and took the two halves.

"Let's go," said the little girl, and then glancing down at her ear of corn, she added: "Dolly's scared too."

Apparently she was reminding him of some previous game in order to divert his attention from the present one.

"That's not a doll, it's an ear of corn," the little boy promptly retorted, violating the rules of the old game for the sake of the new. And now he too was munching away on a cucumber. The little girl had declined her half.

Swearing loudly, Valiko finally managed to drive the goats into the smaller pen and to shut the gate behind them. But no sooner were the goats inside than the goatibex charged forward, scattering them in every direction. Quickly overtaking one of the goats, he knocked her over with a thrust of his horns. She somersaulted headfirst, groaned, but then immediately jumped up and took off as fast as her legs would carry her.

The goats ran along the edge of the fence, pounding the ground with their hoofs and raising a trail of dust behind them. As they ran—sometimes spreading out, at other times bunching together—the goatibex would follow right behind, charging furiously with his horns. Every once in a while he would suddenly stop short in order to choose a better angle of attack. Then, after briefly scrutinizing them with his pink eyes, he would charge forward, scattering the poor animals all over the pen with thrusts of his horns.

"He hates them!" exclaimed the chairman once again, clicking his tongue ecstatically.

"Princess Tamara herself* wouldn't be good enough for him!" shouted the driver from the middle of the pen where he stood enveloped in clouds of dust, like a matador in an arena.

"A fine undertaking, but not for our climate!" shouted the chairman, trying to make himself heard over the stamping and bleating of the goats.

The goatibex grew more and more ferocious, and the goats kept careening around the pen, sometimes converging, at other times scattering in different directions. Finally one of them managed to jump over the fence into the larger pen. The others went hurtling after her, but in their terror they miscalculated the height and fell back onto the ground. Once again they were forced to resume their circular flight around the pen.

"That's enough!" shouted the chairman in Abkhazian. "We're not going to let that swine mutilate our goats."

"I'd be happy to roast and devour that animal at the funeral of the man who dreamed up this whole business!" shouted the driver in Abkhazian as he kicked open the gate into the larger pen. The goats rushed toward the gate, but only succeeded in blocking it as they climbed all over each other, bleating in terror. Without losing any momentum the goatibex made several flying attacks on the mass of writhing bodies, ramming them as best he could through the narrow passageway into the larger pen.

---

* A Caucasian maiden of such legendary beauty that even the devil was haunted by her charms. She is the heroine of Lermontov's poem *The Demon* (Trans.)

It was several minutes before the driver was able to chase him away, and for some time afterwards the goatibex was so keyed up that he kept running around the pen like an angry bull.

"Well, now we can go," said the little girl.

"He sure gave those goats a beating, and all by himself, too!" the little boy announced to his companion. And with that they were off, their tanned and dusty feet padding noiselessly along the dirt road.

We got into the car and drove back to the kolkhoz office. Valiko pulled up in the shade of the walnut tree and we all got out except for the agronomist, who remained dozing inside.

The two old men were still sitting in their former spot, while up ahead next to a brand-new car stood Vakhtang Bochua, sporting a spanking-white suit and a rosy, good-natured smile. Catching sight of me, he comically spread out his arms as if preparing for an embrace.

"So the prodigal son has returned," he exclaimed, "and is welcomed here in the shade of the ancient walnut tree by Vakhtang Bochua and an assemblage of village elders. Bow down and kiss the hem of my Circassian caftan, scoundrel!" he added, beaming with sunny vitality. He was accompanied by a young man who followed his every movement with undisguised admiration.

Suddenly I remembered that he might start speaking to me in Abkhazian and, seizing him by the arm, I drew him aside.

"What's this, my friend, conspiring already?" he asked in eager anticipation.

"Would you pretend that I don't understand Abkhazian," I said in a low voice, "there's been a stupid misunderstanding."

"I get it," said Vakhtang, "you've come to uncover the sinister plots being hatched by the enemies of the goatibex. Well, don't worry, after my lecture goatibexation is going to proceed full speed ahead in the village of Walnut Springs—that I can guarantee," he declared, getting carried away as usual. "Hmm, goatibexation—that's not a bad term,... so don't try stealing it from me before I have a chance to use it."

"Don't worry," I said, "only just keep quiet about my being Abkhazian."

"Yours truly knows how to keep quiet, though it doesn't come easily," he assured me as we started back toward the chairman.

"I hope my lecture will awaken the creative powers of your kolkhoz, even if it doesn't succeed in awakening your agronomist," said Vakhtang to the chairman, at the same time chuckling and winking in my direction.

"This is, of course, an interesting undertaking, Comrade Vakhtang," said the chairman respectfully.

"Which is just what I intend to prove," said Vakhtang.

"What's *your* connection with all this?" I asked. "The last I heard, your field was history."

"Exactly," exclaimed Vakhtang, "and it's my job to consider the historical aspects of the question."

"I don't get it."

"Well, let me explain," he replied with a broad sweep of his hand. "What has been the fate of the mountain ibex down through the ages? He's always been the victim of feudal hunters and the idle scions of the nobility. They tried to exterminate him, but the proud animal refused to submit. He kept retreating farther and farther up the high and inaccessible slopes of the Caucasus, though in his heart he always longed to return to our fertile Abkhazian valleys."

"Oh, come off it!" I said.

"To continue:" he went on, patting himself on the stomach and obviously delighted at his own resourcefulness. "And what has been the traditional role of our plain and unpretentious Abkhazian goat? She has always been the mainstay of our poorest peasantry."

The two old men were listening respectfully to Vakhtang's speech though they obviously didn't understand a word of it. The one with the staff had even forgotten about his hole and was sitting in rapt attention with one ear bent slightly forward in order to catch Vakhtang's every word.

"He's got quite a way with words," said the one with the stick.

"Maybe he's one of them radio fellows," suggested the one with the staff.

"... But she, our humble goat," Vakhtang was continuing, "dreamed of a better fate, or to put it more precisely: she dreamed of an encounter with the ibex... And now, thanks to the efforts of some of our talented specialists (and Abkhazia has always been rich in talent), the mountain ibex has finally encountered our humble domestic goat—plain and unpretentious to be sure, but all the more charming for that."

I blocked my ears.

"Apparently he's been reminded of something unpleasant, see how he's stopped up his ears," said the old man with the stick.

"Probably he's cursing himself for not being able to cure the goatibex," added the old man with the staff. "Why, up in the mountains I used to kill those goatibexes by the hundreds, and now people are cursing themselves over the loss of a single one of them."

"Well, I guess these modern doctors have their problems too," said the old man with the stick.

"... And it is precisely to the intimate details of this encounter that my lecture will be devoted," concluded Vakhtang, now taking out his handkerchief and mopping his perspiring brow.

At this point several disheveled young men walked up to the chairman. They were clearly city types and turned out to be the electricians who had come to install power lines in the village. Right away they launched into an interminably long argument with the chairman. It seemed that some aspect of their work had been omitted from the cost estimate, and now they refused to go back to work until the estimate was revised. The chairman was trying to convince them that this was no reason to walk off the job.

One could not help admiring the skill with which he conducted the argument. It was carried on simultaneously in three languages—Abkhazian, Georgian and Russian—and while addressing the most aggressive member of the group in Russian, the official language, he quickly singled out a quiet Kakhetian* who had hardly opened his mouth and directed most of his remarks to him.

At times the chairman would turn in our direction as if appealing to us as witnesses. Vakhtang would respond with a dignified nod of the head and mumble something to the effect: no

---

* An inhabitant of Kakhetia, a district in eastern Georgia. (Trans.)

doubt about it, you're making a fuss over nothing, my friends; I'll have everything straightened out in the Ministry.

"Do you give these lectures very often?" I asked Vakhtang.

"The requests keep pouring in; I've given eighty lectures in the last two months—ten of them benefits and the rest paid," he reported.

"Well, and what's the response?"

"The public listens and the public understands," he replied obscurely.

"And what's your opinion of all this?"

"Personally, I'm intrigued by his high wool yield."

"Come on, be serious."

"The goatibex needs to be shorn," replied Vakhtang with a straight face. Then suddenly breaking into a smile, he added: "Which is just what I intend to do."

"Well, okay," I said, cutting him short, "I've got to be going."

"Don't be an idiot, stay for a while," said Vakhtang, and lowering his voice, he added: "There'll be some home hospitality after the lecture. For me they'll be happy to slaughter every last goatibex…"

"And what makes *you* so popular?" I asked.

"Oh, I promised the chairman I'd help him get his fertilizer," he replied seriously, "and I really will, too."

"And what's your connection with fertilizer?"

"My dear boy," Vakhtang smiled patronizingly, "everything in this world is connected. Andrey Sharlovich has a nephew who wants to enter the Institute this fall, and your humble servant just happens to be on the admissions board. Why shouldn't the chairman of the district executive committee help a good kolkhoz chairman? And why shouldn't I lend a hand to a young high school graduate? It's all done unselfishly, for the benefit of others."

By now the chairman had succeeded in persuading the workmen to go back to work. He promised to send a telegram right away, instructing an engineer to be sent out from the city to find out who was at fault. The chairman was obviously impatient to be on his way, and the workmen finally plodded off in gloomy fashion, apparently none too satisfied with their partial victory.

I said good-bye to everyone, and the old men politely went through the motions of half rising to see me off.

"The bus has already passed by here, but my driver will take you directly to the highway," said the chairman.

"My driver will be happy to take you too," interjected Vakhtang.

The chairman summoned Valiko and the two of us got into the car.

"I'm afraid he's going to write some sort of nonsense against us," said the chairman to Vakhtang in Abkhazian.

"Don't worry," replied Vakhtang, "I've already given him instructions as to what to write and what not to write."

"Thanks, my dear Vakhtang," said the chairman and then, turning to his driver, he added: "Stop at that restaurant out on the highway and see that he gets plenty to drink. I know these journalists—they can't get along without alcohol."

"Will do," answered the driver in Abkhazian. Vakhtang burst out laughing.

"You don't approve, Comrade Vakhtang?" the chairman asked anxiously.

"My friend, I thoroughly approve," exclaimed Vakhtang, embracing the chairman with one arm. Then, turning in my direction, he shouted above the roar of the motor: "Tell my friend Avtandil Avtandilovich that the promotion of the goatibex is in reliable hands!"

V

The car set off down the road, leaving a trail of dust behind it. The sun had almost set, but there was no letup from the heat.

"Some sort of nonsense against us…" the chairman had said. The way he put it, I might write either for or against them, but whatever I wrote would undoubtedly be nonsense. And now as I reflected sadly on his words, I had to admit that he was not very far from the truth.

With regard to the alleged persecution of the goatibex, for example, I learned from the driver that a short time ago the goatibex had broken loose, run off into the tea fields and gorged himself on tea leaves until, as Valiko put it, he went haywire. He had then raced wildly through the village and at this point some dogs had actually pursued him. The villagers thought he had gone mad and wanted to shoot him, but in the end he had gradually quieted down.

The car leapt onto the highway and a few minutes later pulled up to a pale-blue roadside restaurant. We'll see what luck you have luring me into this place, I thought to myself, at the same time firmly resolving to defend my reputation.

Valiko gazed at me with blue-eyed innocence and asked:

"Shall we stop here for a bite to eat?"

"Thanks anyway, but I think I'll wait till I get back to town."

"You've got a long way to go."

"Still, I'd rather be on my way," I objected, trying to sound as polite as possible. There was something I liked about this fellow with his sparkling blue eyes.

"Just a quick bite," he said, opening the car door. "We'll each order whatever we feel like and pay for it ourselves, Russian-fashion."

What am I worried about, I thought to myself. I know that he's planning to get me drunk, but he doesn't know that I know—which gives me the advantage.

"Okay," I said, "we'll have a quick bite, and then I'll be on my way."

"Why sure, just some *lobio** and greens, that's all."

Valiko locked the car and we went into the restaurant.

The place was deserted except for a party sitting in the corner, squeezed around two tables which had been pushed together. They must have been there for quite a while, since there were half a dozen bottles lying on the floor like emptied cartridge cases. The only woman among the revelers was a blonde, probably a Russian or Ukrainian. She was wearing a sundress with a low neckline and every few minutes she would examine her newly acquired tan. Apparently the tan added to her self-confidence.

Valiko selected a table in the opposite corner—a good choice as far as I was concerned.

The two waitresses sat quietly conversing at a table by the window. Valiko walked up to them, carefully avoiding the middle of the room. Apparently he did not want to attract the attention of the party in the corner. Catching sight of him, the waitresses flashed a friendly smile. The younger one's smile was especially friendly. After greeting both of them in turn, Valiko leaned toward the younger one and began relating some story. The girl continued to smile as she listened to him, her face growing progressively more animated.

"Oh, come on, come on," she seemed to be saying, feebly pushing him away with her hand as she continued to listen with obvious pleasure.

Such fellows always hit it off with waitresses, I thought to myself. But just at that moment her expression changed and I realized that Valiko had started to place our order. I began to get nervous, and now as the waitress happened to glance in my direction, I quickly cried out:

"Don't order any wine for me!"

"How can you have a meal without wine?" said Valiko, turning in my direction and throwing up his hands in despair.

---

* A Caucasian dish consisting of kidney beans topped with a spicy nut sauce. (Trans.)

The party in the corner finally took notice of us, and one of them called out:

"Valiko, come join us!"

"Sorry, old man, I'm afraid I can't," said Valiko, laying his hand on his heart.

"Come on, just for a minute."

"My apologies to all of you and to the lovely lady, but I'm afraid I can't," said Valiko, and backing away respectfully, he returned to our table.

Several minutes later the waitress appeared with an enormous plate of fresh scallions mixed with crimson radishes—the latter peeping through the green scallions like little red beasts. Along with the salad we received separate portions of *lobio* and bread.

"Don't forget the mineral water, Lidochka," said Valiko. And now beginning to relax, I suddenly realized how little I'd had to eat all day. We started off with the *lobio*, which was cold and unbelievably peppery, and then munched away at the radishes and scallions. Each time I bit into one of the spearlike scallions stems, it would spurt forth a spray of its sharp, pungent juice as if in self-defense.

The waitress reappeared with the mineral water and at the same time placed a bottle of wine on the table.

"Nothing doing," I said firmly, putting the bottle of wine back on the tray.

"For God's sake," whispered Valiko, gazing at me with his clear blue eyes in which there was now a look of anxiety.

"What's the matter?" I asked.

"They're treating you," said the waitress, casting a glance at the party in the corner.

As we followed her gaze, our eyes met those of the young man who had greeted Valiko. He was beaming proudly in our direction. Valiko nodded his thanks and shook his head in reproach, whereupon the young man modestly lowered his eyes. The waitress set the wine bottle back on the table and walked off with the empty tray.

"I'm not going to drink any," I said.

"You don't have to drink it, it can just stand there," said Valiko.

82

We started eating again, but the wine seemed somehow to get in the way.

Valiko picked up the bottle of mineral water and asked meekly:

"May I pour you some mineral water?"

"Yes, mineral water's okay," I replied, feeling utterly ridiculous.

Having each downed a glass of mineral water, we went back to work on the *lobio*.

"It's very spicy," observed Valiko, noisily drawing in a mouthful of air.

"Yes, it is," I agreed. The *lobio* did in fact set one's mouth on fire.

"I wonder why the Russians don't like peppers," Valiko queried abstractly, and then reaching for the bottle of wine, he added: "Probably it's the difference in climate."

"Probably so," I agreed, now watching to see what he would do next.

"You don't have to drink it, just let it stand there," said Valiko as he poured out some wine for both of us.

A subtle and fragrant aroma rose from our glasses. It was Isabella wine, a deep crimson in color like pomegranate juice. Valiko wiped his hands on his napkin, finished chewing a radish, and slowly reached for his glass.

"You don't have to drink it, just have a taste," he said, gazing at me with his clear blue eyes.

"I don't want any," I replied, feeling like an absolute idiot.

"May I dig up my father's old bones and throw them to the dirty, stinking dogs, if you don't raise your glass!" he exclaimed in Abkhazian and then abruptly broke off. His enormous blue eyes froze with horror at his own unheard-of sacrilege, and I myself was somewhat dumfounded by this blasphemous outburst.

"The old bones of my father... to the dirty dogs!" he recapitulated and then slumped over the table without a murmur. I grew alarmed.

Don't worry, I thought to myself, you're not going to get high on one bottle. All the more so since you have the advantage of knowing that he wants to get you drunk, while he doesn't know that you know.

We were finishing off the last glass of wine and I still felt completely in control. No one was going to put anything over on me—and actually, Valiko was a nice fellow and everything was turning out quite all right.

The waitress came up with two shish kebabs sizzling on skewers.

"Bring them a bottle of wine from us, and a bar of chocolate for the lady," ordered Valiko. Then with the leisurely finesse of a provincial gourmet he began freeing the still sizzling meat clinging to the metal skewers.

A friendly custom, I thought to myself and suddenly announced:

"Bring them two bottles and two bars of chocolate..."

"The guest said *two* bottles," solemnly confirmed Valiko, and the waitress walked off.

A few minutes later the young man at the other table shook his head in reproach, whereupon Valiko modestly lowered his eyes. The young man then had two bottles of wine sent over to us, whereupon Valiko shook his head in reproach and waved an admonishing finger at him. The young man lowered his head with even greater modesty.

We raised our glasses several times and solemnly toasted our new friends, their old parents, and of course the blonde, who was such a lovely representative of a great people. And now as the rays of the setting sun beat through the window upon her back and glimmered in her hair, simultaneously her face, neck and very bare shoulders were bathed by the shower of compliments emanating from inside the room.

"Let's drink to the goatibex," suggested Valiko somewhat more intimately when it began to appear as if both sides had exhausted their supply of collective toasts.

"Okay, let's drink to him," I said. And we drank to him.

"A fine undertaking, to say the least," said Valiko, and on his lips there appeared a faint smile, the significance of which I did not yet perceive.

"Let's hope it's successful," I said.

"I hear the goatibex is beginning to catch on in Russia, too," he added, the same faint smile still playing about his lips.

"Yes, slowly but surely," I replied.

"It's a matter of State significance," observed Valiko, his eyes now burning with a mysterious blue glitter.

"Yes, it is," I confirmed.

"I wonder what our enemies are saying about the goatibex," he asked unexpectedly.

"They don't seem to be saying anything yet," I answered.

"Not *yet*," he drawled emphatically. "There's more to the goatibex than meets the eye," he added after a moment's reflection.

"There's always more to everything than first meets the eye," I said, trying to grasp what he was driving at.

"But I've got something specific in mind," he said. Then with a piercing glance of his fiery blue eyes he quickly added: "Shall we drink a separate toast to the goatibex's horns?"

"Okay, let's," I said, and we emptied our glasses.

But now for some reason Valiko grew sad. He put down his glass and dejectedly began toying with his shish kebab.

"I have a daughter," he said, gazing up at me with sad eyes, "three years old."

"A wonderful age," I said, doing my best to support this domestic theme.

"She understands everything even though she's only a little girl," he added defensively.

"That's very unusual," I said, "you really are lucky, Valiko."

"Yes," he agreed, "I do everything I can for her. But don't think I'm complaining—I'm happy to do it."

"I understand," I said, although by now I didn't understand a thing.

"No, you don't understand," Valiko retorted.

"What do you mean?" I asked, suddenly noticing that his clear blue eyes had grown glassy.

"May I boil that innocent child in the hominy pot if..."

"Stop it!" I exclaimed.

"Boil her in the hominy pot," he continued pitilessly, "and tear her limbs apart with my own two hands, if you don't tell me what they want with the goatibex—though actually I've already figured it out!" he exclaimed with all the passion of the truth seeker who has kept silent too long.

"What do you mean, *want* with him? Why, meat and wool, of course," I stammered.

"Don't you believe it! They're extracting the atom from his horns," Valiko declared confidently.

"The atom?!"

"I know for a fact that they're extracting the atom, but just how—I haven't figured out," he said with conviction. And once again a mysterious smile hovered about his lips—the smile of a man who knows more than he's willing to let on.

I looked into his good-natured, but now utterly uncomprehending eyes and realized that there was nothing I could do to alter his conviction.

"I swear by my grandfather's ashes that I know nothing of the sort," I exclaimed.

"So they haven't told you people either," exclaimed Valiko in amazement. But what seemed to amaze him was not the fact that people like myself hadn't been informed, but rather that the riddle of the goatibex was proving even more unfathomable than he had imagined.

As we left the restaurant, a warm, starry sky rose darkly above us. The sky was swaying—first coming closer, then retreating. But even as it retreated, it seemed a lot closer than usual. Large, unfamiliar stars blazed in the heavens; strange, unfamiliar thoughts flashed through my mind. It occurred to me that perhaps our friendly drinking bout had brought us closer to the heavens. Some constellation or other stubbornly kept twinkling above my head, and its contours seemed strangely familiar. The goatibex's head!—I suddenly realized to my delight—only one of his eyes was excessively small and myopic looking, while the other was large and kept winking.

"The Goatibex Constellation," I said.

"Where?" asked Valiko.

"Up there," I said, and embracing him with one arm, I pointed to the constellation.

"So they've already renamed it," said Valiko, looking up at the sky.

"Yes," I confirmed, continuing to gaze at the sky. It was a real goatibex's head except that one of his eyes kept winking—but just why it kept winking, I couldn't figure out for the life of me.

"If I've done anything wrong, please forgive me," said Valiko.

"I'm the one who should ask your forgiveness," I said.

86

"If you want to make sure the goatibex is resting comfortably, we can go back and have a look," said Valiko.

"No," I said, "I don't have time for that."

"Well then, if you don't mind, I'll be on my way," he said. "I can still make the movie."

We embraced like brothers, united by our common bond with the goatibex. Then Valiko got into the car.

"Don't wander off anywhere and be sure to get on the Zugdidi bus," he said.

For some reason I almost hoped that he'd have trouble starting the car. But it started up right away, and now he shouted once again:

"Don't take any other bus, wait for the one from Zugdidi!"

For a few minutes I heard the roar of his motor receding into the darkness. Then it died away, and I was left alone in the warm, starlit summer night.

On the other side of the highway there was a park, and beyond the park I could hear the muffled sound of waves breaking against the shore.

Feeling a sudden urge to be close to the sea, I got up and walked across the highway. I remembered that I was supposed to be waiting for the bus, but at that moment it seemed just as logical to wait for it on the seashore.

I entered the park and made my way along one of its tree-lined paths. Silhouetted against the black shadows of the cypress trees were pale phantoms of eucalypti—their broad leaves stirring gently in the cool breeze which blew in from the sea. Every now and then I glanced up at the sky, but there was no cause for alarm. The Goatibex Constellation remained firmly in place.

I was not so drunk as to be oblivious of everything, but just drunk enough to imagine that I was oblivious of nothing.

A couple was sitting on a bench right by the shore. As I started to approach them, they turned their bluish faces in my direction and immediately stopped talking.

"Move over a bit," I said to the boy, and not waiting for an invitation, I sat down between them. The girl gave a timid laugh.

"Don't be afraid," I said peaceably. "I want to show you something."

"Who's afraid?" said the boy, not too confidently as it seemed to me. I ignored his words and turned to the girl:

"Look up at the sky," I said to her in a normal voice, "and what do you see?"

The girl looked at the sky and then at me, trying to make up her mind whether I was drunk or crazy.

"Stars," she said in an overly natural voice.

"No, look up here, right here," I patiently objected, now taking her gently by the shoulder and trying to direct her glance toward the Goatibex Constellation.

"Let's go, they'll soon be locking up," the boy said gloomily. He was obviously trying his best to get out of a bad situation.

"Locking up where?" I asked, politely turning in his direction. It pleased me to know that he was afraid of me—all the more so since in this case my manners had been impeccable.

"At the tourist camp," he replied.

It suddenly occurred to me that there might be some mysterious and perhaps even dangerous connection between the Goatibex Constellation and the tourist camp.*

"Strange that you should mention the tourist camp," I said, apparently more sternly than necessary. The boy did not reply, and I looked at the girl. She had wrapped her woolen sweater snugly around her shoulders as if to escape some cosmic chill emanating from my person.

I looked up at the sky. The bright dotted outline of the goatibex's face was swaying—sometimes coming closer, at other times moving farther away. Every now and then his big eye would wink. I was sure that this winking had some special significance, but exactly what it was, I couldn't for the life of me figure out.

"Goatibex watching is a favorite pastime for tourists," I said.

"Perhaps we should be on our way," said the girl quietly.

"Well, go ahead," I said calmly, at the same time letting them know that I was disappointed in them.

Seconds later they had disappeared from sight. I closed my eyes and began to ponder the significance of the goatibex's winking. The sea's refreshing coolness and the steady pounding of the

---

* In his drunken haze the narrator makes a false association between the Russian word for "ibex" *(tur)* and the abbreviation for "tourist," as it appears in the word "tourist camp"*(turbaza)*. (Trans.)

88

waves lulled my senses and from time to time I would sink into oblivion, only to emerge seconds later like a piece of rock rising from the foam of an outgoing wave.

Suddenly I opened my eyes and saw two policemen standing before me.

"Let's see your papers," said one of them.

I mechanically reached into my pocket for my passport* and handed it to him. Then I closed my eyes. When I opened them again, it seemed as if a considerable amount of time had passed and I was surprised to see the two policemen still standing there.

"You're not allowed to sleep here," said one of them, returning my passport.

"I'm waiting for the Zugdidi bus," I said, closing my eyes once again or, rather, easing up on my efforts to keep them open.

The policemen chuckled.

"Do you have any idea what time it is?" one of them asked.

I felt something unpleasantly abnormal about my left arm and quickly raised it, only to discover that my watch was missing.

"My watch!" I exclaimed, jumping to my feet. "Someone's stolen my watch!"

By now I was completely awake and completely sober. The sun had already come up and there was a raw wind blowing in from the mountain pass. The rollers were breaking heavily against the shore. Standing on a strip of beach across from us was an elderly tourist, doing his morning calisthenics. As he lowered himself slowly, painfully slowly on his long thin legs, I couldn't help wondering if he would ever get up again. But having rested at the bottom of his deep knee bend, he managed to raise himself in slow, wobbling fashion. Once fully erect, he stretched out his arms and froze in position as if he were trying to regain his balance. Or perhaps he merely wished to listen to the inner workings of his body after this strenuous exertion.

The policemen had also been following the old man's movements and now, no longer worried on his account, one of them turned to me and asked:

---

* Most Soviet citizens are required to carry internal passports which contain their name, address, age, nationality, marital and civil status as well as their complete employment record. (Trans.)

"What make was your watch—a Pobeda?"*

"No, a Doxa—a Swiss watch," I replied bitterly, though not without feeling a certain pride at the magnitude of my loss.

"Who was with you?" asked the other policeman.

"I was alone," I replied cautiously.

"We'll go back to the station and file a report," said the policeman who had taken my passport. "Then if it turns up, we'll notify you."

"Okay, let's go," I said. And we set off.

I felt very sad at the loss of my watch, which I'd come to think of almost as an old friend. It had been a high school graduation present from my uncle, and I had worn it all these years without anything ever happening to it. It was waterproof, shatterproof, antimagnetic, and its black shiny face gleamed like a miniature night sky. Several times during my student days at the Institute I had accidentally left it in the dormitory washroom, but the cleaning lady or one of my classmates had always returned it to me. Thus, over the years I had somehow come to believe that in addition to all its other virtues it was also theftproof.

"Do you have an import authorization form for your watch?" asked one of the policemen.

"How could I?" I replied. "It was war booty, my uncle brought it back in forty-five."

"Do you remember the serial number?" he asked, continuing with his questions.

"No," I answered, "but I'll recognize it without that."

We had cut diagonally through the park and come out onto a quiet, unfamiliar street. This street—as indeed every street in town—was lined with one-story houses mounted on long, rickety piles. The residents of this town were occupied solely with the building of such houses. And once they had built one, they would immediately begin selling it or exchanging it at additional cost for some other house which was supposedly more attractive—though in what way, one could never figure out, for all of these houses were as much alike as peas in a pod. The owners themselves scarcely had time to enjoy them, since for half the year they would rent them out to tourists in order to accumulate enough

---

* The Russian word for "victory." (Trans.)

capital to begin frantically building a new house with even longer and ricketier legs. In this town a man's whole worth was defined by the phrase: "He's building a house."

A man who's building a house is an honest man, a decent and deserving man. A man who's building a house is a man who keeps himself busy in his spare time, a man who has put down roots. If something happens, he's not going to take off—which means he's trustworthy. And a trustworthy man is a man you can invite to weddings and funerals, a man who would make a good son-in-law or a good father-in-law. In short, he's a man you can do business with.

I mention all this not because it was here that my watch was stolen, but because such has always been my opinion of the town. Actually it's not even a question of personal gain in this case, since the house or, more accurately, the process of building the house is merely a symbol for something else. If, for example, it were agreed that from this day forth a man's worth was to be measured by the number of peacocks he had raised, everyone in town would immediately start raising peacocks and would soon be swapping them back and forth, feeling their tails and boasting about the size of their eggs. Man's passion for self-esteem can take the strangest and most varied forms. The form itself is immaterial as long as it catches the eye and represents a sufficiently large investment of time and energy.

Passing through a creaking wicket gate, we entered the well-kept grounds of the local police station. A spreading mulberry tree stood in the center of the luxuriant green lawn, and placed conveniently under its leafy branches were some benches and a solidly anchored table for backgammon or dominoes. Between the lawn and the picket fence there was a row of young apple trees heavily laden with fruit. This was the most hospitable-looking police yard I had ever laid eyes on, and I could easily imagine the police chief sitting here with a flock of penitent criminals, putting up preserves on a fall afternoon.

We followed the well-beaten path which led up to the building and went inside. A policeman was sitting behind a wooden partition in the middle of the room, and right by the door a young couple was seated on a long bench. The girl reminded me of the girl I had seen the night before, except that now she wasn't wearing a sweater. I gave her a questioning look.

One of my police escorts left the room. The other took a seat on the bench, and turning to me, he said:

"Well, go ahead and file your complaint."

Then he took a good look at the young couple on the bench and glanced questioningly at the policeman seated behind the partition.

"Picked up wandering around without any papers," the latter explained matter-of-factly.

The girl had turned her head and was now gazing in the direction of the open door. Once again she reminded me of the girl from the night before.

"Where's your sweater?" I asked her, suddenly overcome by a desire to play detective.

"What are you talking about—what sweater?" she said with a haughty glance in my direction and then turned her head once again toward the door. The boy looked up in alarm.

"Excuse me," I mumbled, "I mistook you for someone else."

From her voice I realized that she was not the same girl. I have a bad memory for faces, but voices I remember very well. Taking out my notebook, I walked over to the partition and began thinking about how I would phrase my complaint.

"You can't use that for an official statement," said the policeman behind the partition as he handed me a clean sheet of paper.

I gave in, now realizing once and for all that my notebook was not destined for use on this assignment.

"Please let us go, comrade policeman," the boy pleaded dully. "You'd think we'd committed a crime or something."

"As soon as the captain arrives, he'll decide what to do," replied the policeman from behind the partition. His tone was clearly conciliatory, and the boy said nothing more. Through the open windows one could hear the distant scraping of the caretaker's broom and the chirping of birds.

"How much longer do you expect us to wait?" the girl asked angrily. "We've already been sitting here for an hour and a half."

"Now don't get smart, young lady," said the policeman without raising his voice or changing his position. He sat there at his table, with his cheek resting on one hand and a sad, sleepy look on his face. "The captain's out making his rounds. There's been a rape case," he added after a moment's reflection, "and here you are wandering around without any papers."

"Now that's what I call a brilliant association!" the girl retorted sarcastically.

"You're too smart for your own good," dolefully remarked the policeman without raising his voice. And he continued to sit there as immobile as ever, with the same sleepy look on his face.

When I had finished writing up my complaint, the policeman indicated with a glance that I should leave it on the table. Just at that moment the door opened at the back of the partitioned-off area and a tall, thickset man with slightly stooped shoulders entered the room, thoughtfully stroking his broad, handsome face with one hand.

"Well, here's the captain," the policeman exclaimed joyfully, now jumping up and yielding his seat to the captain.

"I wonder why we didn't hear his car pulling up," the girl remarked impudently and then turned once again toward the door.

"What's the trouble?" asked the captain, taking his seat and gazing somberly at the girl.

"They were picked up wandering around without any papers," reported the policeman in a loud, clear voice. "They were spotted on the shore at about four a.m. She claims that she didn't want to wake up her landlady, and her escort's staying at the other end of town."

"Comrade captain," the boy was about to begin, but the captain cut him short:

"You run and get your passport, and she can stay here as security."

"But there aren't any buses at this hour," the boy objected.

"Never mind, young man, run along," said the captain, now turning with a questioning glance toward me.

"Here's his statement, comrade captain," said the policeman, pointing to the table. The captain leaned forward and began reading my statement. The policeman who had escorted me to the station now stood at attention, ready to fill him in with any necessary details.

"Now don't get upset, I'll be right back," the boy whispered to the girl and quickly departed. The girl made no reply.

93

Through the open windows came the scraping sound of the caretaker's steadily approaching broom and the irrepressible warbling of birds. The captain's lips moved slightly and, looking up at me, he asked:

"Do you have any identification?"

"It was war booty," I replied, assuming that he was referring to the watch, "a gift from my uncle."

"What's your uncle got to do with it?" The captain asked with a frown. "Show me your passport."

"Oh," I said, handing him my passport.

"He was sleeping down by the shore," interjected my policeman, "and after we woke him up, he said his watch had been stolen."

"How strange," said the captain, gazing at me with curiosity. "According to your statement you were waiting for the Zugdidi bus, and yet they found you sleeping down by the shore. Don't tell me you were expecting the bus to come out of the sea?!"

The two policemen chuckled.

"The Zugdidi bus comes by at eleven in the evening, and we found him on the shore at six a.m.," observed my escort, as if presenting some new challenge with which to test the captain's ingenuity.

"Perhaps you were waiting for the return bus?" the captain suddenly surmised. One could tell that he was trying his best to make sense of my story and was suffering in the process.

"Yes, the return bus," I said for no good reason, except perhaps to put the captain's mind at rest.

"Well, that's another matter," said the captain and then, holding out my passport, he asked: "Where do you work?"

"I'm a reporter for *Red Subtropics*," I replied, extending my hand to take the passport.

"Then why weren't you staying at the hotel?" asked the captain. And now puzzled anew, he took back my passport and opened it for a second look. "This sort of thing makes a bad impression," he commented, and clicking his tongue, he added: "What am I going to tell Avtandil Avtandilovich?"

Good Lord, I reflected, they all seem to know each other around here!

"Why do you have to tell him anything?" I asked. That was all I needed—to have the editor find out about my stolen watch! There would be all sorts of questions, suspicions—and in general, who wants anything to do with people who get into trouble?

"This does create a bad impression," the captain declared thoughtfully. "You spend the night in our town and you lose your watch... What is Avtandil Avtandilovich going to think?"

"You know," I said, "I think I may have left it at Walnut Springs."

"Walnut Springs?" the captain gave a start.

"Yes, I was there on an assignment in connection with the goatibex."

"Oh, I've heard, an interesting undertaking," observed the captain, now listening attentively.

"I think I may have left my watch there."

"Then we'll call them up right away," said the captain, his face brightening as he reached for the receiver.

"No, don't bother!" I cried, taking a step forward.

"Aha," said the captain, slapping his hands together. His face lit up with satisfaction at his own clever surmise. "Now I understand, they were making toasts..."

"Yes, that's it, making toasts," I confirmed.

"By the way, Vakhtang Bochua was out there too," interjected my escort.

"So they were making toasts," the captain went on with his explanation. "You ended up presenting your watch to one of them, and they presented you with a cigarette case," he concluded, now beaming triumphantly in my direction.

"What cigarette case?" I asked, failing at first to see the connection.

"One of those silver ones," the captain cheerfully elaborated.

"No, they didn't give me anything in return," I said.

"But they must have," said the captain, amiably contradicting me. "Or at least they must have promised to give you something later on... But why are you standing? Have a seat." And taking a package of Kazbek cigarettes from his pocket, he asked: "Do you smoke?"

"Yes. Thank you," I replied, taking a cigarette. The captain gave me a light and then lit up his own cigarette.

At this point the policeman who had been standing behind the partition went out through the back door. My policeman continued to stand in place, though now partially supporting himself against the window sill.

"Last year I happened to be in Svanetia,"* said the captain, directing a cloud of smoke at the ceiling. "The local police had a dinner in my honor; we ate and drank and afterwards they presented me with a deer. Now what on earth would I want with a live deer? On the other hand, to refuse it would have been considered a mortal insult. So I accepted their gift, promising to send them two cases of cartridges in return. And I did send them, as soon as I got home."

"And you took the deer?" I asked.

"Of course," he answered. "I kept it at home for a week, and then my son took it off with him to school. 'We're going to make it into a goatibex,' he tells me. 'Fine,' I tell him, 'do whatever you want with it. There's no way we can keep it at home.' "

The captain took a long draw on his cigarette. Good-natured complacency was written all over his broad, handsome face. I was glad that he had forgotten about my watch; I would have had a rough time explaining what had happened to Avtandil Avtandilovich.

"The Svans are excellent cooks," the captain continued to reminisce, "but that arrack spoils everything." He looked at me and frowned. "A thoroughly distasteful drink—although I suppose," he added in a conciliatory tone, "it's all a matter of what you're used to."

"Yes, I suppose so," I replied.

"But that Isabella they have at Walnut Springs is as strong as bull's blood…"

Yours isn't bad either, I thought to myself.

Suddenly beginning to chuckle, the captain asked: "Did you get to meet that sleepy agronomist?"

"Yes, I did," I replied. "Why *does* he sleep so much?"

"He's quite a character," said the captain, chuckling again. "It's some sort of sickness he has. But despite all his sleeping, he's

---

* A district in northwest Georgia, inhabited by an ancient Caucasian people, the Svans. (Trans.)

still our number-one tea specialist. There's no one in the district who can match him."

"Yes, their tea fields are really magnificent," I said, suddenly calling to mind the picture of Gogola bending over the green, luxuriant bushes.

"Last year there was a bit of excitement out at their kolkhoz. Someone walked off with their safe."

"Their safe?"

"Yes, their safe," said the captain. "I went out there myself to investigate. Someone managed to steal it, but they couldn't get it open. The sleepy agronomist helped us find it. He's a very smart fellow... But you know, Isabella really is a treacherous wine," the captain continued, not wanting to digress too far from his main topic. "You gulp it down like lemonade and only later does it begin to hit you."

He looked at me, then at the girl, and said to her:

"You're free to go, young lady, only next time see that you don't stay out so late."

"I'll wait for my friend here," she said, turning her head brusquely toward the door.

"You can wait for him out in the yard. It's a nice morning—the birds are singing," said the captain and then added sternly: "And in the future don't let yourself be picked up by casual strangers. All right now, get along with you!"

The girl went out without saying a word. The captain nodded in her direction and remarked:

"They're offended when we take precautionary measures, and yet later on they themselves come running in to complain: 'He raped me! He robbed me!' Who he is or where he's staying, she doesn't have the slightest idea. And as to how she happened to be with him, she won't say a word." The captain turned to me with an offended look in his eyes.

"I suppose they're too young to know any better," I said.

"That's just the point," said the captain.

Out in the yard the birds were chirping away for all they were worth, and now the scraping of the caretaker's broom could be heard right outside the front entrance.

"Kostya," said the captain, turning to my escort, "go on out and water the front lawn and the sidewalk before it gets hot."

"Yes, sir! Comrade captain," replied the policeman.

97

"And tomorrow you'll go to the circus," added the captain, his words bringing the policeman to a sudden halt by the door.

"Yes, sir! Comrade captain," the policeman repeated joyfully and then walked out.

"What circus?" I asked without stopping to reflect that this might be some sort of code word and, if so, my question would not be appreciated.

"The circus has arrived in town," replied the captain matter-of-factly, "and we're rewarding some of our best men by assigning them guard duty there."

"Aha," I nodded in comprehension.

"He's a good man—smart and hard-working," said the captain, glancing in the direction of the door. "Twenty-three years of service and now he's even building himself a house."

"Well, I guess I'll be on my way too," I said, rising.

"What's your hurry?" asked the captain, and glancing down at his watch he declared: "The Zugdidi bus isn't due in for another hour and forty-three minutes."

I sat down again.

"But do you know what goes best with Isabella?" he asked, glancing at me with good-natured cunning.

"Shish kebab," I replied.

"I beg your pardon, dear comrade," objected the captain with obvious satisfaction. And now, having apparently concluded that I was an amateur who would have to be taken thoroughly in hand, he came out from behind his partition.

"Isabella should be served with stew meat and *adzhika*.* Especially meat from the loin—that's where you get your chops," he explained, slapping himself on the back. "But the leg isn't bad either," he added, hesitating somewhat, as if he wanted above all to be fair or in any case did not want to be accused of any culinary bias.

"Meat served with *adzhika* makes you thirsty," said the captain, now halting in front of me. "You may not even feel like drinking any more, but your body demands it!" he added, joyfully flinging up his hands as if to say: there's nothing you can do about it, once your body demands it.

The captain resumed his pacing.

---

* A spicy Caucasian condiment. (Trans.)

"But white wine doesn't go well with meat," he suddenly cautioned, halting and looking anxiously in my direction.

"What does it go well with?" I asked eagerly.

"With fish," he replied, "Goatfish," the captain bent back one finger, "horse mackerel, mullet, or a fresh-water fish—mountain trout, for instance. Mm-m-m," murmured the captain with satisfaction. "And all you need with the fish is damson sauce and some greens—nothing else." And grimacing at the mere thought of any other side dishes or appetizers, he mentally brushed them aside with an energetic sweep of his hand.

The captain and I continued talking for a while until finally, when I was convinced that his thoughts had wandered sufficiently far afield from my watch, I shook his hand and said good-bye. But just as I was heading for the door, he called out:

"Here's your statement; take it with you."

He handed me the statement, and then apparently noticing that I didn't enjoy being reminded of my missing watch, he added:

"Don't worry, nothing's going to come of it. The authorities regard gift giving as a harmless local custom. It's quite acceptable in this part of the country."

After this short legal briefing I said good-bye to him once again and finally left the building.

The freshly watered front lawn of the police station lay sparkling under the still cool morning sun. The policeman was energetically applying his hose to a young apple tree. Whenever a jet of water hit the tree, there would be a hollow rustling sound and a mighty quiver of gratitude would pass through its leaves and branches. Then from the still trembling leaves the water would come flying forth in a rainbow-colored spray.

The girl was sitting under the mulberry tree, keeping an eye on the front gate as she awaited her sweetheart's return.

Out on the street I tore up my statement and threw it into a refuse container. I just barely made my bus and spent the entire return trip outlining my future article on the goatibex of Walnut Springs. It occurred to me that my grief over the loss of my watch would inject a note of pathos into my article, and this thought somewhat consoled me.

99

VI

I decided to tell everyone at home that my watch had been stolen from my hotel room. My uncle took the news very badly—which rather surprised me since I had no idea he would still remember the present he had given me so many years ago. I should add that my uncle was reputed to be one of the city's best taxi drivers, and about two days after my return he pulled up in front of our building with a cab full of passengers. Leaving his passengers in the cab, he came inside and began questioning me:

"Well, how did it happen?"

"I was sharing a room with someone and when I got up in the morning, both the man and my watch were gone," I explained sadly.

"Well, what did he look like?" asked my uncle, already thirsting for vengeance.

"He was asleep when I came in," I replied.

"Don't be silly," said my uncle. "Obviously he was only pretending to be asleep. Well, what happened after that?"

"When I got up in the morning, both the man and the watch were gone..."

"You've already said that," he broke in impatiently. "Do you really mean to tell me that you didn't notice what he looked like?"

"He was under the blanket," I said firmly, not wanting to give him anything more concrete to go on. Knowing how determined my uncle could be, I was afraid that he might start rounding up all his more suspicious-looking passengers and herd them into the newspaper office for me to have a look at.

"He had his head under the blanket in this heat?!" my uncle exclaimed. "Why that alone should have made any intelligent person suspicious. Well, and where was your watch?"

"It was lying under my pillow," I said firmly.

"How come?" he asked, frowning. "Why would you bother to take it off when it's unbreakable?"

I didn't take it off, I was about to object, but I caught myself just in time.

"Well, what did the hotel management say?" asked my uncle, not letting up on his questions.

"They said I should have turned it over to them for safe-keeping," I replied, remembering that such was the procedure at the public baths.

Sooner or later he would probably have tripped me up with his questions, had it not been for his abandoned passengers, who now began raising a fuss out front. First they blew the horn, then they started banging on our apartment window.

"The next time I pass through that town I'm going to stop off at that hotel and give 'em hell!" was my uncle's parting shot as he went dashing out onto the street.

He was so grief stricken over the loss of my watch that I began to wonder if he hadn't perhaps been planning to reclaim it at some future date. But then it occurred to me that the loss of a gift must inevitably strike the gift giver as a form of ingratitude. For when a person gives us something, he is making a deposit, as in a savings account, from which he hopes to collect a small but fixed rate of interest. And when the gift is lost, he feels doubly cheated: for not only has he lost his original deposit, but his small percentage of gratitude as well.

Fortunately, an opportunity to pass through the ill-fated town did not immediately present itself and my uncle gradually calmed down. But I seem to be jumping ahead, and I need first to go back and describe the day of my return from Walnut Springs. True, this day has little to recommend it, but describe it I must if my story is to be complete.

The clock on the municipal tower was just striking nine when I entered my office. Platon Samsonovich was already at his desk and as he looked up, apparently startled to see me, his freshly starched shirt crackled, as if galvanized by the mere touch of his wizened old body.

I could tell that he had been struck by some new inspiration, since his flights of creativity were always celebrated by the donning of a clean shirt. Thus, although it might be objected from the standpoint of personal hygiene that Platon Samsonovich changed his shirts rather infrequently, in terms of intellectual creativity he was changing them constantly. Indeed, his mind seemed always to be operating at fever pitch.

"You can congratulate me," he exclaimed. "I've come up with a new idea!"

"What sort of idea?" I asked.

"Just listen and I'll tell you," he replied, fairly beaming. He reached for a piece of paper and began writing down some formula, explaining it as he went along. "I propose that we crossbreed the goatibex with the long-haired Tadzhik goat, thus obtaining:

$$\text{Goat} \qquad \text{Ibex}$$

$$F_1 \text{ Goatibex} \qquad \text{Tadzhik Goat}$$

$$F_2 \text{ Goatibex}$$

Of course the jumping ability of the second-generation goatibex will be somewhat diminished, but he'll have twice as much hair. Pretty good, eh what?" exclaimed Platon Samsonovich, now discarding his pencil and gazing up at me with sparkling eyes.

"Where are you going to get a Tadzhik goat?" I asked, vaguely aware of some hidden danger lurking in his eyes.

"I'll go to the agricultural administration office," he said, rising. "They ought to support our efforts. Oh, how was your trip?"

"Okay," I replied, sensing that his thoughts were elsewhere and that he was inquiring merely out of politeness.

He dashed to the door, but then suddenly returned to his desk, picked up the piece of paper on which he had written his new formula, and put it away in the top desk drawer. He locked the drawer with a key, jiggled it just to make sure, and then put the key in his pocket.

"Keep quiet about this for the time being," he instructed me in parting, "and write up your article. We'll submit it right away."

There was a note of superiority in his voice—the natural superiority of the creative engineer over the ordinary technician. I sat down at my desk, took out my pen and reached for some clean sheets of paper. But I couldn't think where to begin, and taking out my notebook, I started leafing through it, even though I knew there was nothing in it.

Anyone reading our paper would have supposed that all but the most ideologically backward collective farmers were busy raising goatibexes and nothing else. In the village of Walnut Springs, however, this was not quite the case. Realizing that it would be naive to make any direct attack on the goatibex, I decided to adopt Illarion Maksimovich's approach—that is, to support the project as a whole, while making considerable allowance for local conditions. I was still deliberating on how to begin, when the door opened and a girl from the mail and supply room walked in.

"You have a letter," she said, eyeing me strangely.

I took the letter and opened it. The girl remained standing in the doorway and only when I looked up at her, did she reluctantly leave the room, closing the door slowly behind her.

The letter was from Russia, from a former colleague at the youth newspaper. Word had reached them of our interesting undertaking, and the editor wanted me to write an article for them on the goatibex. For although I had left them, they still thought of me as one of their own—one whom they had nurtured and helped on his way. Such were the editor's exact words, cited ironically by my friend. It was only in his private correspondence, I might add, that my friend ever indulged in irony.

The way the editor put it, it would appear that I had been nurtured by the youth newspaper and then left it of my own accord.

Nor was the remaining portion of the letter any more to my liking. Here my friend reported that he sometimes saw *her* in the company of the major. There were rumors that they had gotten married—but this wasn't yet definite, he added in closing.

Of course it's definite, I thought to myself as I put down the letter. I've noticed that people sometimes try to soften unpleasant news, not so much out of sympathy for us, the recipients, as out of sympathy for themselves. For who wants to have to utter the words appropriate to such occasions, to exhort us to keep a stiff upper lip or, even worse, to face up to reality?

I don't want to exaggerate. The old wound didn't reopen, nor was I about to slit my throat. In fact, all that I experienced was a dull ache, the sort of ache which rheumatics feel at the onset of bad weather. I decided, however, to put even this suffering to good use and to let it, along with my missing watch, contribute to the pathos of my article.

I have a theory that one's personal failures can contribute to success if only one knows how to make use of them. I have had a lot of experience with failure and consequently have learned to put it to good use.

One should not, of course, take my theory too literally. If, for example, someone steals your watch, this doesn't mean that you should immediately start learning to tell time by a sundial. Nor should you suddenly imagine yourself one of the proverbial few for whom time does not exist.

But all this is beside the point. What's important is the emotion you feel—that righteous but unproductive fury which is an inevitable by-product of failure. This is fury in its purest form, and while it's still seething in your blood, you should quickly channel it in the right direction and not let yourself get carried away by trifles in the process—which unfortunately is what most people tend to do.

Let us imagine, for example, a certain individual, who in a state of noble fury decides to make the most daring and momentous phone call of his life—and on a pay phone at that. Before he has even been connected, however, the telephone swallows his only coin. Quivering with rage, the man begins tugging at the receiver hook as if it were the ripcord of a parachute that refused to open. Then, even more illogically, he tries to thrust his head into the coin return which, being no larger than a matchbox, obviously cannot accommodate a human head. But never mind that, let us suppose that he does manage to thrust his head into this miserable aperture; what good will it do him? Even if he should happen to catch sight of his lost coin, he will hardly be able to scoop it out with his tongue.

Finally, having spent all his fury in this senseless pulling and tugging, he leaves the phone booth and, quite unexpectedly perhaps even for himself, takes a seat in a shoeshine stall. To look at him now, you would think that he was merely out for a stroll and had decided to stop and get a shoeshine on the way. Just as if his noble fury had never existed! And what is particularly revolting is the way he keeps fiddling with the new laces he has just purchased from the shoeshine man—first checking their tips and then comparing them for length. He continues to sit there for a long time, his lips slightly extended as if he were whistling to himself, and on his face the calm, businesslike expression of a fisherman letting out his nets or of a peasant fingering the old sack in which he plans to take his grain to the mill.

Ah, whither art thou fled, noble fury?

Another individual, having reached this exalted state, suddenly starts dashing after a little boy who has accidentally hit him with a snowball. Well, even supposing it was no accident, why on earth should a grown man go out of his way to chase a little boy, especially when there is no hope of catching him. For of course this little boy knows all of the yards and alleyways of the area like the palm of his hand. And to make things more interesting, he purposely slows down just enough so the man can keep him in sight.

Having squandered all his fury in this unexpected chase, the man suddenly comes to a halt in front of a warehouse and begins to watch some truckers unloading huge barrels from the back of a truck. So intently does he watch them, in fact, that one would think he had come running up for this very purpose. After a while, when he catches his breath, he even starts giving them advice. No one listens to him, of course, but they don't interrupt him either. Thus, from a distance it might appear as if the truckers were actually working under his supervision, and if he hadn't come running up in time, who knows what chaos might have resulted. Finally the barrels are rolled into the cellar and the man walks away appeased, as if all that had happened were a normal part of his daily routine.

Ah, whither art thou fled, noble fury?

As I was lost in these reflections, the door opened and once again the girl from the mail and supply room walked in.

Fazil Iskander

"I've brought you some paper," she said, placing a ream of paper on Platon Samsonovich's desk.

"Thank you," I replied. This time I was happy to see her; she had roused me from my daydreams.

"Well, what's the news from Russia?" she asked with affected casualness.

"They want an article on the goatibex," I replied equally casually.

She gave me a long, quizzical look and then walked out.

Once again I settled down to work. The goatibex emerged as the star of my article, far outshining everyone else. The village of Walnut Springs rejoiced at his presence, though unfortunately, due to local climatic conditions, the goatibex had taken a dislike to the local she-goats. I was just putting the finishing touches on this charming tableau when the phone rang. It was Platon Samsonovich.

"Listen," he said, "couldn't you hint in your article that some kolkhoz workers are already beginning to talk about the long-haired Tadzhik goat?"

"What are they supposed to be saying?" I asked.

"Something to the effect that while they're happy with the goatibex, they want to keep moving forward. Otherwise these people here at the agricultural administration will start dragging their feet and refuse to cooperate."

"But it's all your own idea," I objected.

"Never mind," said Platon Samsonovich, sighing wearily into the receiver. "I'll worry about the recognition later. Right now it would be better if the idea came from the masses. That will encourage these people here to take action."

"I'll think about it," I said and then hung up.

I knew that certain sections of my article would not be to his liking, and in order to gain approval for these sections, I decided to support his new idea. But this was easier said than done. For thinking back over all the people I had met at Walnut Springs, I realized that not one of them could possibly have referred to a Tadzhik goat, except perhaps for Vakhtang Bochua—and Vakhtang hardly qualified as a kolkhoz worker. After much deliberation I finally decided to refer to the animal myself, at the end of the article and in such a way as to make it appear that the crossbreeding of

106

the goatibex with the Tadzhik goat was a logical next step in the development of our livestock industry. "The time is not too far away," I wrote, "when the goatibex will encounter the long-haired Tadzhik goat—an event which will mark yet another significant breakthrough for our Michurin school of biology."

I read over what I had written, placing the commas as best I could, and then turned the article in to the typist. Having struggled with it for almost three hours, I was utterly exhausted. At the same time, however, I felt like a diplomat who has just pulled off a brilliant coup. For thanks to my skill and finesse, the goatibexes had been given their due and the chairman had emerged unscathed.

I left the office and went to have lunch at an outdoor café located in the courtyard of one of our seaside restaurants. I sat down at a table under a palm tree and ordered a bottle of Borzhom mineral water, some *chebureki*,* and two cups of Turkish coffee. After finishing the *chebureki*, I furtively wiped my hands against the shaggy trunk of the palm—the waitress having neglected as usual to bring any napkins. Then I settled back and began sipping the strong, thick coffee. Once again I pictured myself as a diplomat—an exceptionally skillful and experienced one at that. The hypnotic rustling of the palm leaves, the hot coffee, the cooling shade of the palm tree, the old men peacefully clicking their worry beads—all these things gradually drove the goatibex from my mind, and I sank into a blissful torpor.

At the next table the dentist Solomon Markovich was holding forth before a group of old-timers. Long ago, sometime before the war, his wife had slandered and deserted him, and from that time on he had started drinking and generally going to seed. He was a great favorite with the café regulars, who were always buying him drinks. Although their sympathy for him was probably genuine, still it is always pleasant to see someone who is even more unfortunate than ourselves. At the moment, he was relating parables from the Bible to his elderly Muslim audience, interspersing them with examples from his own life.

---

* A spicy lamb dumpling popular in southern Russia and the Caucasus. (Trans.)

"... So they say to me: 'Solomon Markovich, we're going to put you on the bottle.' And I say to them: 'Why bother? You might as well put me right on the floor?'"

Every time Solomon Markovich caught sight of me, he would say:

"Young man, I've got quite a story for you, quite a story! Why, I'll tell you the story of my life from the cradle to the grave."

After this I usually had no choice but to order him a cognac and a cup of Turkish coffee. Every once in a while, however, I refused to go along with this ritual, either because I was pressed for time or was simply not in the mood to listen to someone else's troubles.

I finished my coffee and returned to the office. On the way back to my desk I stopped off to pick up my article from the typist, only to be informed that the editor had taken it.

"You mean he actually came in for it himself?" I asked, feeling a sudden, inexplicable anxiety and, as usual, getting caught up in irrelevant details.

"He sent his secretary in for it," she replied without letting up on her typing.

I went into my office, sat down at my desk and began to wait. The editor's haste was not entirely to my liking since there were several points in my article that I felt needed to be worded more clearly and precisely. And in any case, I had wanted Platon Samsonovich to read the article first.

I sat there awaiting my summons. Finally the secretary came running in and announced in a frightened voice that the editor wished to see me. Although her voice always sounded frightened when relaying the editor's requests, on this occasion I found it particularly disturbing.

I opened the door to Avtandil Avtandilovich's office and saw, somewhat to my surprise, that Platon Samsonovich was there too.

The editor was sitting in his usual pilot's pose. He had turned off the engine but was still in the cockpit. The greasy blades of the fan looked like the giant petals of some tropical flower—most likely a poisonous one. One could easily imagine that Avtandil Avtandilovich had just flown over the locale of my assignment and was now making a comparison between what he had seen and what I had written.

Next to this tall, dashing pilot the diminutive Platon Samsonovich looked at best like a mere mechanic. And at the moment he looked like a mechanic who had made a mistake. Approaching Avtandil Avtandilovich's desk, I felt a sudden chill emanating from his presence, as if he were still enveloped in the high-altitude atmosphere from which he had just descended.

So great was this atmospheric chill that I felt I was beginning to grow numb. I tried to shake off this humiliating sense of paralysis, but nothing came of it, perhaps because he kept silent.

Suddenly it occurred to me that my article was thoroughly confused and mistaken. And now as all my errors came vividly to mind, I could only wonder how I had managed to overlook them before. Particularly unpleasant was the realization that I had even confused Illarion Maksimovich's name, referring to him instead as Maksim Illarionovich.

Finally, when the editor sensed that I had reached the necessary degree of paralysis, he proclaimed in a voice calculated to maintain this paralysis:

"Your article is hostile to the goatibex."

I looked at Platon Samsonovich; Platon Samsonovich looked at the wall.

"Moreover, you tried to disguise your hostility," added Avtandil Avtandilovich, obviously enjoying my discomfort. "At first even I was taken in by it," he continued. "Some of your similes and comparisons are quite good... Nonetheless, your article represents a revision of our basic position."

"Why a revision?" I asked, my voice rising from some great depth where patches of unfrozen consciousness still remained.

"And what's all that nonsense about local climatic conditions—the goatibex and the microclimate? What do you think we're raising—oranges and grapefruit?"

"But he really does refuse to have anything to do with the local goats," I said in an agitated voice, trying to disarm him with hard, cold fact. And suddenly I realized beyond the shadow of a doubt that there had been no mistakes in my article and that I had referred to Illarion Maksimovich throughout by his right name.

"Which only means that they haven't yet learned to handle him properly, that they haven't explored all possibilities... And you let yourself be taken in by them."

"It was that chairman Illarion Maksimovich who pulled the wool over his eyes," interjected Platon Samsonovich. And turning to me, he added: "After all, I did tell you that your article should be organized around the theme: 'Tea is fine, but meat and wool are better.' "

"And you can be sure," the editor interrupted him, "that if we give these chairmen any loopholes like this business with the microclimate, they'll all start screaming that *their* microclimate is unsuitable for raising goatibexes... And to have this happen now, just when the whole country is taking an interest in our undertaking...!"

"Well, aren't *we* and *they* supposed to be the same thing?" I blurted out without stopping to reflect. Well, now I'm done for, I thought to myself.

"There, you see, that just goes to show what backward notions you have," replied the editor in a surprisingly mild tone and went on to ask: "By the way, what was that nonsense about the long-haired Tadzhik goat—where on earth did you get that from?"

I noticed that he had calmed down right away. Apparently I was responding just as he had intended.

Platon Samsonovich pursed his lips, and red splotches appeared on his temples. I kept silent. Avtandil Avtandilovich cast a sidelong glance at Platon Samsonovich, but didn't say a word. Apparently he wanted to give both of us time to feel the full weight of my fall. Once again I began to think that everything was lost, though it occurred to me that if he were going to fire me, he should have seized upon my last words. Yet for some reason he had chosen not to.

"Redo it in the spirit of full-scale goatibexation," said the editor with a meaningful look as he flung the manuscript in Platon Samsonovich's direction.

How does he know that word, I wondered, now waiting for what would come next.

"I'm going to transfer you to the cultural section," said the editor in the tone of a man who is doing his utmost to be fair. "You know how to write, but you don't have any knowledge of life. We've decided to have a contest for the best literary piece on the goatibex. You're to take charge and see to it that it's conducted in a serious, professional manner... That's all I have to say."

Avtandil Avtandilovich turned on the fan, and his face gradually began to stiffen. And now as Platon Samsonovich and I made our way out of his office, I had a fearful vision of his air-borne plane swooping down on us with a volley of machine-gun fire. Only after the heavy office door had slammed shut did I regain my composure.

"It's fallen through," said Platon Samsonovich as we started down the corridor.

"What's fallen through?" I asked.

"The Tadzhik goat," he replied. Then rousing himself from his daydreams, he added: "You didn't handle it right. You should have let the idea come from one of the kolkhoz workers."

"Okay, okay," I replied. I was fed up with the whole business.

"Goatibexation! The way he throws words around!" grumbled Platon Samsonovich, nodding in the direction of the editor's door.

We returned to our office and I began gathering up the contents of my desk drawer.

"Don't feel bad, I'll manage to have you transferred back here later on," promised Platon Samsonovich. "Oh, by the way, is it true that the paper you used to work for has asked you to send them an article?"

"Yes, it's true," I replied.

"Well, if you're not in the mood, I could do it for you," he said, brightening.

"Fine. It's all yours," I replied.

"I'll do it this evening," he said. By now he had thrown off the last traces of his despondency and, nodding once again in the direction of the editor's office, he muttered: "Goatibexation! Some people play around with words; others get things done."

Later that same afternoon a terrible thing happened to me as I was walking along the main street of town. A man wearing a brand new suit was standing near me on the sidewalk, gazing into the display window of a department store. Behind the window stood several mannequins. These mannequins were dressed exactly like the man—so much so, in fact, that I couldn't help thinking how alike they were. But no sooner had this thought flashed through my mind than one of the mannequins

111

began to move. I was stunned though at the same time I had enough common sense to realize that this must be some sort of hallucination. Mannequins don't move—we haven't yet come to that.

But before I could collect my thoughts any further, the mannequin that had begun to stir suddenly defied all laws of nature by turning on its heels and walking calmly away. I was still recovering from this shock, when suddenly the other mannequins began to stir. They stirred for a moment, then they too turned on their heels and followed calmly after the first one.

Only after they had all come out onto the street did I realize that this conspiracy of mannequins was merely some sort of optical illusion which had been intensified by my fatigue, nerves, and who knows what else. For what I had taken to be a department store was actually a glass partition, and the people whom I had taken for mannequins had merely been standing on the other side of the glass wall.

I need a breath of fresh air, otherwise I'll go mad, I thought to myself as I hastily directed my steps toward the sea.

I have always hated mannequins. Ever since childhood the very sight of them has filled me with loathing and disgust, and even now I fail to understand why such an abomination is tolerated. For a mannequin is quite a different thing from a scarecrow, which does at least have some character of its own. And while the scarecrow may frighten children for a short time and birds for a somewhat longer time, still it does not really offend us. There is, on the other hand, something brazen and vile in the mannequin's striking resemblance to man.

Do you really believe that the mannequin's only function is to model a suit of clothes? Don't be naive! The mannequin wants to prove to us that it is possible to be a human being even when lacking a soul. Moreover, he urges us to follow his example. And by always modeling the latest fashions, he seems cynically to suggest that it is he who points the way to the future.

But we can't accept his future because we want our own, human future.

When I gaze into a dog's eyes, I find something resembling a human look, and I respect this look. I see the millions of years that separate us, but at the same time I see that the dog has a soul, a certain shared humanity. The dog seems to sense this common humanity and to respond to it. Undoubtedly it is the dog's capacity to respond to us as humans which evokes a similar responsiveness in us and, in fact, strengthens our own humanity. For when a dog barks joyfully at our approach, we instinctively respond and our hand reaches out to pat him.

I admire the parrot's talents—its vocal cords and its mechanical memory—but the parrot is far behind the dog. The parrot is interesting and exotic, but the dog is beautiful.

We are often willing to use an imprecise word to designate the essence of something. But even if we manage to be precise in our designation, the essence itself may change, while its designation, the word, still continues to be used, preserving not the essence, but only its outward form, just as an empty pod preserves the rounded contours of the long-discarded peas. Errors of terminology or of perception—and usually we are guilty of both—lead in the end to a confusion of concepts. And in the last analysis, a confusion of concepts is but a natural outgrowth of our indifference—our insufficient concern for the essence of the concept, or insufficient love. For is not love the highest form of concern?

Sooner or later we are forced to pay for our indifference. And only then, still nursing our bruises, do we begin to call things by their right names. In the meantime we continue to confuse parrots with prophets simply because we have given little or no thought to the subject of man and the source of his greatness. Why—because we have little respect for ourselves, for those around us, and for life itself.

About three days later I happened to be eating lunch in the same outdoor café, when who should appear but Vakhtang Bochua. Dressed in a spanking-white suit and as rosy-cheeked as ever, he was a radiant vision of pink and white. Accompanying him were an elderly gentleman and a woman who was dressed with the gay abandon of a fortuneteller. Catching sight of me, Vakhtang halted.

"How did the lecture go?" I asked.

"The collective farmers were moved to tears," he replied with a smile. "Oh, and by the way, you owe me a bottle of champagne."

"What for?" I asked.

"Don't tell me you haven't heard!" he exclaimed in surprise. "It was yours truly who dragged you out from under the wheels of history. Avtandil Avtandilovich wanted to bid you farewell, but I told him it would be over my dead body."

"What was his reaction to that?" I asked.

"He accepted the fact that this was one place where the wheels of history were going to get stuck," said Vakhtang. Then, giving his mighty stomach a loving pat, he added: "You've been granted a stay of execution."

He stood before me ruddy, portly, smiling and invulnerable. He himself seemed rather amazed at his own boundless capacities and now was eagerly trying to think of something else with which to impress me.

"Do you know who they are?" he asked with a slight nod in the direction of his companions. The latter had already taken a table and from their seats were casting fond glances at Vakhtang.

"No," I answered.

"My friend, Professor (he gave his name), the world-famous mineralogist, and with him his favorite student. By the way, he's given me a collection of Caucasian minerals."

"How come?" I asked.

"I don't know myself," replied Vakhtang, throwing up his hands in mock despair. "I guess he just likes me. I've been taking him around to different historical sites."

"Vakhta-a-ang, we miss you," the favorite student drawled capriciously.

Even the professor was gazing in our direction with an affectionate smile. He was casually garbed in linen trousers and sandals, and his long legs protruded from under the table like those of some lanky, absentminded adolescent.

"And that's not all," said Vakhtang, still smiling. And shrugging his shoulders as if to express his amazement at the vagaries of human behavior, he added: "He's even promised to leave me his library."

"Well, see that you don't do him in for the sake of his wealth," I said.

"What do you mean!" protested Vakhtang with a smile. "Why, he means as much to me as my own father..."

114

"Greetings to our golden youth," interjected Solomon Markovich, suddenly appearing from out of nowhere. He stood before us—small, wrinkled and alcoholically preserved for life in his quiet but persistent sorrow.

"My dear Vakhtang," said Solomon Markovich, "I'm an old man. I don't need a hundred grams of vodka; a mere fifty will do."

"That you shall have," said Vakhtang, and taking Solomon Markovich's arm in lordly fashion, he directed him to his table.

"And here is one more of our archaeological rarities," said Vakhtang by way of introduction. And pulling up a chair for him, he added: "Please welcome the wise Solomon Markovich."

Solomon Markovich sat down and in a quiet and dignified manner began:

"Yesterday I was reading a certain book; it's called the Bible."

He always began this way, and it now occurred to me that his approach to life was a good illustration of my theory of failure and how to make the most of it. For from the great failure of *his* life he had extracted one small but enduring triumph: the privilege of daily libations at others' expense.

VII

I had been quietly at work in the cultural section for about a month. The furor in connection with the goatibex campaign had not yet died down, but by now it no longer bothered me. I had gotten used to it, just as one gets used to the sound of waves pounding against the shore.

The high-level regional conference to promote the goatibex-ation of our Republic's kolkhozes had already taken place, and although a few critical voices had been raised against the meas-ure, they were quickly drowned out by the clamor of the trium-phant majority.

Our paper's contest for the best literary piece on the goatibex was won by an accountant from the Lykhninsky Kolkhoz. He had written a satiric ode entitled "The Goatibex and the Hardheaded Chairman," the last stanza of which read as follows:

I take up my pen in praise of the goatibex,
For despite what the hardheaded chairman may say,
The animal's meat and its beautiful horns
Have made their mark and are here to stay.

To appreciate the biting effect of this stanza one needs to know something of the poem's background. For the poem was actually based on a real-life incident.

On a certain kolkhoz a goatibex had almost gored the kolkhoz chairman's small son. According to Platon Samsonovich, the little boy had frequently teased and made fun of the defense-less animal, taking advantage of his father's position to do so. The goatibex had given the child a good scare, it seemed, but had not

116

inflicted any serious injuries. Nonetheless, acting at the insistence of his infuriated wife, the chairman had ordered the local black-smith to saw off the animal's horns.

It was at this point that the secretary of the village soviet had written in to us. Platon Samsonovich was outraged by the incident and the very next day went out to the kolkhoz to see for himself what had happened.

It turned out that everything the secretary had written was true. Platon Samsonovich even brought back with him one of the goatibex's horns (the other, as the kolkhoz chairman was embar-rassed to admit, had been dragged off somewhere by a dog). Every one of our paper's employees came trooping into Platon Samsonovich's office to see the famous goatibex horn; even the phlegmatic typesetter made a special trip up from his presses to have a look at it. Platon Samsonovich was delighted to be able to show it off and, in doing so, he would direct everyone's attention to the traces left by the blacksmith's barbarous saw. The horn was brown and heavy like the tusk of some antediluvian rhinoceros, and the head of the information section, who also happened to be the chairman of the paper's trade union committee, suggested that we turn it over to a local craftsman and have it converted into a drinking horn for use at staff picnics.

"It could easily hold three liters," he said, scrutinizing the horn from every angle. His suggestion, however, was indignantly rejected by Platon Samsonovich.

In connection with this same incident Platon Samsonovich wrote a satirical sketch entitled "The Goatibex and the Hard-headed Chairman," in which he gave the kolkhoz chairman a merciless going-over. He even suggested to the editor that his sketch be supplemented by a photograph of the dishonored animal, but after some reflection Avtandil Avtandilovich decided to let it go with the sketch.

"They might take it the wrong way," he replied, though exactly who the "they" was, he did not bother to explain.

So it was that when the Lykhninsky accountant submit-ted his poem of the same title, it received Platon Samsonovich's full backing and was virtually assured of first place, since Platon Samsonovich was the most influential member of our contest jury and its only technical expert. Nor did the editor have anything against the poem; he merely observed that the last two lines would have to be revised in such a way as to pay tribute to the goatibex's wool along with his meat and horns.

"We don't yet know which is going to be more important for the economy," he said and then suddenly came out with his own improved version of the last stanza, which was now amended to read as follows:

> I take up my pen in praise of the goatibex,
> For despite what the hardheaded chairman may say,
> The animal's meat, its wool and its horns
> Have made their mark and are here to stay.

The author had no objection to Avtandil Avtandilovich's slight revision and shortly afterward the poem was even set to music. The tune was a popular one, or at least so one would judge from the fact that it was frequently played on the radio. It was also sung on stage by an amateur choir from the tobacco factory—the choir consisting in this case of members of the Municipal Opera and Choral Society. Scarcely recognizable in their folk dress, the latter sang under the direction of the now rehabilitated Pata Pataraya, a performer of Caucasian dances who had been popular in the thirties.

As for the horn, it remained in Platon Samsonovich's office, surmounting a pile of unfiled papers as a visible reminder of the need for vigilance.

Most of my time in the cultural section was spent processing our readers' letters (usually complaints about the poor performance of their village social clubs) and their attempts at verse.

The verses were devoted largely to the goatibex and, strangely enough, the majority of them came pouring in after the contest was already over. Many of them even bore the heading: "Entered for the next contest," though in fact no such contest had ever been announced.

Some contributors, and especially the elderly and the retired, would let it be known in an accompanying letter that they had been well provided for by the State and hence had no need for any prize money. If, however, they would go on to add, there were some young staff writer who would be willing to make whatever corrections were necessary for the poem to be printed, then his modest efforts would not go unrewarded; for all forms of labor should be remunerated, etc., etc. At first I was annoyed by these references to a *young* staff writer, but eventually I got used to them and no longer paid any attention.

In my initial replies to these contributors I politely hinted that creative writing requires a certain amount of talent and even some familiarity with literature. After a few days, however, Avtandil Avtandilovich called me into his office and informed me that in the future I would have to be more tolerant. Pointing to a particularly candid section of one of my more recent replies, which he had underlined with red pencil, he said:

"You can't tell a person that he hasn't any talent. It's our responsibility to educate people's talents and to encourage their creative efforts, especially those of ordinary workers."

By this time I had managed to discover Avtandil Avtandilovich's one great weakness. This powerful individual would freeze like a rabbit when under the hypnotic spell of a cliché. And if at the moment he happened to be promoting some new political cliché, it was literally impossible to win him over by logical argument. Instead, one had to fire up his enthusiasm with some other cliché—one that was even more up to date than the first. Thus, when he began talking about the education of talent and the creative efforts of ordinary workers, I was immediately reminded of the old cliché about not flirting with the masses. I didn't have the courage to quote it, however, nor did it quite seem to fit this particular situation.

After my meeting with the editor I began replying to our contributors with even less enthusiasm than before. Clenching my teeth and fuming with rage, I would cynically advise them to study the classics—and especially Mayakovsky.*

During this same period I had several out-of-town assignments, and each time I returned with an article, I knew in advance which sections would be to the editor's liking and which would not. And for those sections which were destined

---

* A major Russian poet of the early twentieth century and the leading exponent of Russian Futurism. In official circles Mayakovsky has consistently been regarded as Russia's greatest poet of the Revolution. (Trans.)

for deletion I did what little I could, making them stylistically as attractive as possible.

Things were proceeding pretty much as usual when something occurred which, while in no way related to the goatibex, was nonetheless to have a certain influence on my life.

One evening I was sitting with some friends on top of the sea wall, gazing down at the double stream of smartly dressed people who kept passing one another on the street below. And perhaps because of their constant movement—their jostling and intermingling—there was an air of excitement about them which conveyed itself to us.

Black pants, pointed shoes, a dazzling white shirt, and a pack of Kazbek cigarettes stuck in one's belt like a cowboy pistol—such was the summer attire of our southern Don Juans.

The evening promised nothing special, nor were we expecting anything out of the ordinary. We were simply sitting and enjoying ourselves, gazing idly at the passers-by and making the extravagant comments men usually make on such occasions.

Then *she* appeared—a young girl in the company of two elderly ladies. As they passed right beside us on the sidewalk, I managed to catch a glimpse of her charming profile and luxuriant, golden hair. She was a most attractive girl. Only her waist struck me as overly slender; there was something old-fashioned about it—something from the era of stays and corsets.

She was politely and submissively listening to what one of the ladies was saying. But I didn't have much faith in her submissiveness; it seemed to me that a girl with such full lips was not likely to be very submissive.

I followed her with my eyes until she and her companions had disappeared from sight. Fortunately, my friends hadn't noticed her. They had been so absorbed in watching the street below that they had failed to see what was right under their noses. I continued to sit there for a while, but my friends' conversation no longer reached me. I was so immersed in my thoughts that their voices seemed to be coming from far away, as if across a broad expanse of water.

I couldn't get the girl out of my mind. I wanted to catch sight of her again and as quickly as possible. Not that I feared any competition from our local dandies. With their languorous gait and silly cartridge belts stuffed full of half-empty cigarette packs, they were simply not her type—of that I was sure. No, in this case the challenge lay elsewhere. And what a pleasant challenge it would be to deliver her from under the overly protective wing of two elderly ladies.

Without further delay I took leave of my friends and started off down the street. The chances of finding her in such a mass of humanity seemed very remote, but by now she was fixed in my mind. And once a person is fixed in your mind, however slightly, you can be sure that somehow, somewhere your paths will cross. Well, I thought to myself, if this is the way I feel about this girl, I must finally be cured of the old one. The major had proved a good doctor, and now in my willingness to be afflicted once again I saw the sure sign of my recovery. I began to look for her.

Although I knew that I would eventually find her, I hadn't the slightest idea what would happen after that. For the moment, I simply wanted to convince myself that she had in fact appeared before me and was not merely a figment of my imagination.

Suddenly, as I was approaching the small pier used by our local fishing and excursion boats, I saw her in the distance, leaning against the guardrail and gazing into the water. She was wearing a simple white blouse and a very full skirt which made her tiny waist look even tinier. She had the sort of figure which can be cut with a pair of scissors, as we say in Abkhazian.

Sitting on a bench nearby were the two ladies with whom she had walked so submissively along the embankment.

In connection with these ladies I should point out that many people have a distorted view of our region and of the Caucasus in general. Most of the rumors about girls being kidnapped, carried off into the mountains, etc., etc., are sheer nonsense. Nonetheless they continue to circulate and many people believe them.

Be that as it may, the girl's lady companions were now sitting so close to her that if any abduction had been attempted, they could easily have reached out and grabbed the edge of her skirt without even rising from their seats. This same skirt was now flapping widely and freely around her legs like the flag of some independent but thoroughly reliable power.

Still debating what to do next, I made my way to the end of the pier. Then as I turned around and started back, I decided to throw caution to the winds and come to a halt beside her. In so doing, I would take advantage of the one tactical error committed by her escort: her seaward flank had been left unguarded.

The sea was my ally, and now as I made my approach, a light breeze began blowing at my back like a friendly hand urging me on to some daring act. All of a sudden a gust of wind lifted her skirt so high that I had the feeling she would fly off before I could reach her. I hastened my steps involuntarily. But now, without even bothering to look, she clapped down her skirt with her hand—as if she were merely closing a window to keep out a draft. Or perhaps this is the way one collapses a parachute. Although I myself have never parachuted and, needless to say, never intend to, for some reason the image of a parachute, and specifically a collapsed one, persists in my mind.

But how was I actually going to strike up a conversation with her? Suddenly it came to me! I would pretend that I too was a tourist. For some reason tourists usually trust each other more than they do the local residents. And as for her being a tourist—this was apparent at a glance.

And so I walked up and stood beside her. I stood there quietly and unobtrusively, as if I just happened to be out for a stroll and had decided to stop and have a look at the Black Sea splashing here in this out-of-the-way spot where there were no tourists to appreciate it. And not wanting to give any grounds for suspicion, I didn't even glance in her direction.

Right beneath us, gently knocking against the iron ladder of the pier, was a small skiff which belonged to the fishing boat anchored a short distance away. It was this skiff that she was looking at. In retrospect one could say that she was staring Fate straight in the eyes, but at the time I didn't know this. I noticed only that she was gazing at the skiff somewhat pensively, as if perhaps she were thinking of using it to make a getaway from her companions. Needless to say, I would have been happy to offer my services, if only as rower.

I stood beside her, growing stiffer by the minute and realizing that the longer I waited, the harder it would be to start a conversation.

"I wonder what kind of boat that is," I finally mumbled, turning toward her—but only halfway, at a forty-five degree angle. It would be hard to imagine a more idiotic question. The girl gave a slight shrug of her shoulders.

"How strange," I said, pursuing the same foolish line of thought, as if the sight of a skiff tied up at a pier were something to be marveled at. "They say that the border's very close," I continued boldly, at the same time wanting to bang my head against the guardrail.

"Why strange? Do you think they might be smugglers?" she asked with enthusiasm.

"At the tourist home they told us that…," I began confidently, without the slightest idea as to what I was going to say next.

Just at that moment there was a shuffling of boots, and two men began descending the iron ladder. One of them was carrying a large wooden basket covered with a towel; the other had a sack slung over his shoulder.

I broke off in midsentence and laid a finger to my lips.

"How exciting," whispered the girl. "What are they going to do?"

I gave a slight shake of my head as if to indicate that nothing good could be expected from such men. The girl bit her lip and huddled even closer to the guardrail.

The man with the basket jumped into the bow of the swaying skiff, hopped over the front and middle seats and sat down in the stern, placing the basket between his legs. Before I could collect myself, he raised his dark, ruddy face in a smile and nodded in my direction. He was one of the fishermen with whom I had gone out on my first assignment some time before. His name was Spiro.

"Greetings to our friends from the press!" he called out, his white teeth flashing.

Blushing involuntarily, I gave a slight nod in his direction. But it was too late to shut him up.

"You sample our fish, but write about the goatibex," he shouted and then, taking in both of us at a glance, he added: "An interesting undertaking, to say the least…"

"How's it going?" I asked limply, realizing that it would be ridiculous to try to keep up the pretence any longer.

"I've just put some of our bonus money to good use, as you can see." He pulled back the towel covering the basket; it was filled with bottles of wine.

"We're going to overfulfill the plan, though we haven't yet landed any golden fish,"* he added, glancing at the girl with shamelessly transparent eyes. "*Kalon karitsa* (a nice-looking girl)!" he shouted in Abkhazian, leaning back in his seat and bursting into laughter. Obviously he had thoroughly sampled the wine before buying it. And now, suddenly remembering something, he started off on a new tangent:

"Oh, Miss, ask him to sing you the goatibex song. He sings it very well; they're all singing that song and every time they sing it, they raise their glasses to the goatibex."

Finally his companion pushed off from the pier and began to row. Spiro continued to horse around, pretending at one point that he was about to drown himself before our very eyes—we being too blind and foolish to appreciate this exceptional personality who was still in our midst.

"Don't keep your readers in suspense!" he cried from a distance as the skiff began to fade into the sea's wavering darkness.

The girl seemed to have taken it all very well and now, seeing the friendly smile on her face, I began to relax.

"What's this goatibex he was talking about?" she asked after the boat had disappeared from sight.

"Oh, it's just a new animal," I replied casually.

"That's funny, I wonder why I've never heard of it before."

"You soon will," I said.

"And you sing a song about this new animal?"

"You might say that I hum along."

"Are they already singing it in Moscow?"

"Not yet, I don't think."

"It's time we left," came an unexpected voice from the rear.

We turned around. The two ladies had gotten up from the bench and were eyeing me with open hostility.

"We're on the beach every day," she said as if finishing a sentence. Then she meekly walked over to her companions and took them by the arm.

I bid all three of them a polite farewell and quickly walked off. I crossed the shore boulevard and made my way home along

---

* In one of Pushkin's well-known fairy tales a golden fish grants a number of wishes to a kindly fisherman who has freed her from his net and returned her to the sea. (Trans.)

a deserted side street where I was unlikely to run into any of my friends. I didn't want anyone or anything to detract from my present state of euphoria. And as I walked along, happily reflecting on her last words, it seemed perfectly natural to interpret them as an indication of her desire to see me again.

The next day at the office I was fairly bursting with joy at the thought of our future meeting. Not wanting to be caught in any indecent display of emotion, however, I decided to dampen my joy somewhat by spending the entire day answering letters from our readers.

At five o'clock sharp I locked the door to my office, left the building and caught the first bus headed for the beach. The bus was jammed with people, and the smell of sweat lay heavy in the air.

Upon arrival at the beach I was immediately enveloped in the soft, soothing music which came from the loudspeaker. Somehow the music always made it easier to undress, forming as it did a sort of fluid transition between land and sea.

Feeling somewhat excited, I started off down the beach, peering under tents and umbrellas along the way. All around me was a profusion of multicolored bathing suits, healthy-looking tans of every possible shade, and languid, complacent poses worthy of the ancient Greeks.

Suddenly I began to feel that I was in no great hurry to find her; for as long as I continued to search for her, I still had the right to observe and admire my surroundings. It even seemed to me that yesterday's impressions had begun to wear off, apparently dulled by this carnival of seaside color. And knowing from experience that any overflow of feeling would be self-defeating, I was happy to note that for the moment at least, my feelings remained completely under control.

Whenever I met a girl I liked, I would foolishly overwhelm her with an avalanche of my most exalted feelings. As a result the girl would usually take fright or even be offended. Perhaps the very strength of my feeling made her wonder if she had not underestimated her own charms and somehow overlooked the wealth of resources buried within her. And if such were the case, her first priority, metaphorically speaking, was to reevaluate these resources, stake them off or, at any rate, not yield them up to the first bidder.

Whatever the reason, as soon as the avalanche came hurtling down on top of her, I would promptly be relegated to a second-string position. Eventually I would tire of this and become interested in some other girl. And even though I knew I should be more cautious and restrained, each time the process would repeat itself: the avalanche of feeling would come hurtling down of its own accord, and the girl would jump out from under it completely unscathed—or at most with a slightly rumpled hairdo.

Reflecting on all this, I could not help but rejoice at my present state of calm. By this time, however, I had walked the length of the beach, and now as it appeared that I was not going to find her, my mood began to deteriorate. I even tried walking along the water's edge in order to have a closer look at those who were bathing, but she was not here either.

Noticing that the afternoon sun was beginning to fade, I slowly began to undress. As long as I was here on the beach, I might as well take a swim. Standing nearby was a photographer dressed in white shorts beneath which gleamed the bronze and sturdy legs of the seaside entrepreneur. At the moment, he was photographing a woman whose head had just emerged from the foam of an incoming wave.

"Just one more shot, Madame."

And now the wave retreated, revealing the arms and torso of this sea-sprung Venus. She lay resting on her hands, which were firmly implanted in the sand.

"Okay...get set!"

He proceeded so slowly and painstakingly—in the manner of some old-time resident of St. Petersburg—that a group of young tourists sitting nearby suddenly burst out laughing.

The photographer got ready to take another picture, and once again the group got ready to laugh. The woman tried to simulate an expression of bliss, but could not seem to rid her face of its slightly preoccupied look. Apparently the enveloping foam was no more inspiring than soapsuds.

"Okay ... here goes," the photographer suddenly announced with a cautionary glance at the young people.

But they laughed all the same, and now even the photographer himself began to smile. It was a long, sunburnt smile, and one could tell that he sympathized with these young people. Yes, he understood that they were still young and foolish, but they too should understand that his profession was no more laughable than many other things in this world, and in general one should have the patience to live a little before passing judgment on such matters.

I went into the water, but instead of feeling refreshed, I felt only hunger and vexation. Suddenly I remembered that I'd forgotten to eat lunch—something which rarely happened with me.

Now even the beach was beginning to get on my nerves. All the flabby cardplayers with their thin, arthritic legs, the athletes with their tightly flexed but utterly superfluous muscles, the local Don Juans with their foolish and completely unwarranted arrogance, and finally the women with their supposedly irresistible charms displayed supposedly for the sake of a tan.

I quickly got dressed and left the beach. I took a bus into the center of town and from there made my way home on foot—hungry, tired and annoyed. But just as I was about to open the front door, I discovered that I had lost my key. I went through all my pockets, but the key was nowhere to be found. And now I realized that I was in for a streak of bad luck. It's always that way with me. Things either go beautifully or else I can't seem to do anything right. Apparently the key had fallen out of my pocket when I was dressing on the beach. Or at least so I hoped, since this was the only place where I could even begin to look for it.

Cursing my own bad luck and everything else under the sun, I walked to the nearest bus stop and once again set off for the beach. By now the bus was a lot less crowded; it was too late for anyone to be going swimming.

At one of the stops along the way the bus driver left the bus and returned five or ten minutes later with some hot meat pastries which could be seen gleaming faintly through a grease-soaked paper bag. Leisurely munching his pastries, he continued along for two more stops and then once again left the bus. Across from the bus stop was a beer stand, and here he ordered a chaser for his pastries. As the passengers grumbled in timid protest, I began studying the tall wooden building which stood next to the beer stand. It was a branch of the People's Court, and it occurred to me that our driver might even take it into his head to wander inside and listen to some case. He probably would have had the gall to do so, beer mug and all, but for the time being he stood quietly sipping his beer.

I remained in my seat by the rear door and absentmindedly began kneading my ticket between my fingers. Finally, when my patience had come to an end, I flicked the ticket through the open door. But at that very moment a ticket inspector entered the bus through the forward door and began checking people's tickets. I should have gotten off the bus at this point and started looking for my ticket, but I was too embarrassed to do so; I was sure everyone would think I was trying to get away.

Finally the inspector got to me. I tried to explain what had happened, but my story sounded ridiculous even to me. As for the inspector, he obviously was not going to let me think for a moment that he believed me.

I got down from the bus and accompanied by good-natured chuckles from the passengers seated closest to the door, I began combing the ground for my ticket. But the ticket was nowhere to be found. I refused to be easily discouraged, however, and now began calculating the probably trajectory of its flight. But in the spot where it should have landed there was nothing; undoubtedly it had been carried away by the wind. As I continued to search, the inspector stood by the door with a pained and weary look on his face—one of those looks I've never been able to stand. It was as much as to say: how can you expect to find what you haven't lost?

The passengers must have decided that I had earned my deliverance for suddenly they all began to speak up in my defense, assuring the inspector that they had seen me throw the ticket away. Apparently feeling it best to yield to public opinion, he let the matter rest, merely giving me a short reprimand as he left the bus.

Our driver had finally finished his beer, and now as he slammed the forward door shut and briskly started up the motor, we all felt a wave of gratitude which, needless to say, we would not have felt, had he proceeded along his route as he was supposed to.

I sat back and tried to resign myself to my fate, knowing from experience that once I'd fallen upon a streak of bad luck, there was nothing I could do but try to get through it with as few losses as possible.

Finally we arrived at the beach. I got off the bus and made my way to the entrance booth, only to discover that I was three kopecks short of the ten kopecks admission fee. Apparently I'd forgotten to take any money with me when I left home that morning.

It has always bothered me that one has to pay to go to the beach—as if the sea were some creation of the city authorities.

"Come on through, you were already here," said the lady ticket collector, noticing my hesitation. I looked up and saw an elderly woman with a kind, smiling face. How amazing that she had happened to remember me.

I walked onto the beach, so heartened by this bit of good luck that I felt a great burst of energy welling up inside me. Perhaps the wheel of fortune was beginning to turn. And suddenly I was sure that I would find my key, although up till now I had scarcely entertained any such hope. After all, from a strictly logical point of view my chances of finding it were almost nonexistent. For even if I had lost it on the beach, by now hundreds of people would have passed by the spot, and any one of them could have picked it up.

Be this as it may, not only did I find my key, but I actually caught sight of it from a distance. Yes, this small, almost luggage-size key lay flashing in the sand in the very spot where I had undressed to go swimming. No one had picked it up or even stamped it into the sand. As I picked up the key and was putting it in my pocket, I happened to glance in the direction of the sea, and now all of a sudden I was seized by a strange, indescribable sensation. I saw before me the warm, azure expanse of the sea, radiant in the setting sun; the laughing face of a girl who kept looking around as she made her way into the water; a boy sitting in a lifeboat with his strong, suntanned arms resting on the oars; and the shore itself, dotted with hundreds of people. And this whole scene was so softly and clearly illuminated and so full of peace and goodness that I froze with happiness.

This was not the sort of happiness which can be evoked by memory, but another, higher and extremely rare form of happiness which mere words are almost powerless to convey. It was the sort of happiness one feels in one's blood and tastes on one's lips.

It seemed to me at this moment as if all these people had come to their own beloved sea after a lifetime's long and difficult journey, a journey from afar which had been made since time immemorial. And now at last, the people were happily reunited with their sea, and the sea with its people.

This extraordinary state of mind lasted for several minutes and then gradually began to fade. But even after the original intensity was gone, there remained a certain aftertaste—like the heady sensation which lingers on after our first gulp of early morning air.

I don't know what brings on this feeling, but I have experienced it often—or perhaps not so terribly often, if I consider my life up to now. Usually it has come upon me when I'm alone—in the mountains, in a forest or by the seashore. And who knows, perhaps it is a presentiment of some other, more fully realized life which could or even will exist in the future.

Still reflecting on all this, I got onto the bus and made my way home—this time, I might add, forgetting to take any ticket at all.*

Later that evening I wandered around the city, hoping that I might run into her. I was terribly eager to see her again, although at the same time I was beginning to dread our next encounter. Several times that evening I felt an abrupt sinking sensation in the pit of my stomach—the same sensation one feels in an airplane when it hits an air pocket—but each time it turned out to be a false alarm; it was not she but someone else.

I had just wandered onto the small pier used by our local boats when suddenly I saw her. Somehow it had never occurred to me to look for her here; and yet here she was, standing in almost the very same spot where she had stood the evening before.

My first impulse was to run away, and it was only with great difficulty that I managed to resist the temptation. I started walking toward her along the well-lighted pier, but for some reason she didn't see me. She seemed to be buried in thought, or perhaps she simply didn't want to see me. In any case, I had just drawn level with her and was about to turn back, when suddenly our eyes met and she smiled—or more accurately, her face lit up with joy. And like some sudden gust of wind, her radiant smile swept away all the tension and fatigue I had accumulated in the course of the day.

It is not so often that people are genuinely happy to see us, or at least not so often as we would like. And even when a person

---

* In the Soviet Union local buses often operate on the honor system. The passenger drops his coin into a fare box located at the back of the bus and takes his own ticket without any supervision from the driver or other attendant. (Trans.)

is happy to see us, he usually tries to hide the fact, either because he's afraid of appearing overly sentimental or else of offending the others present, at whose appearance he cannot rejoice. Thus it is that sometimes we're not really sure whether a person is happy to see us or not.

An excursion boat suddenly pulled up to the pier, and as if by some previous agreement we got on board. I don't remember what we talked about; I only remember that we stood leaning against the rail, gazing down at the water, just as the night before we had stood by the guardrail on the pier. Only now it seemed as if the pier had separated from the shore and was speeding into the open sea. I gazed down at her face and was strangely moved by the expression of tenderness which filtered through her tanned and slightly peeling skin.

Later on she wanted something to drink and we made our way along the dark and narrow passageway to the stern, where the snackbar was located.

We ordered some lemonade which turned out to be cold and bubbly like champagne. It had been a long time since I had drunk lemonade, and it suddenly occurred to me that no champagne had ever tasted as good as this lemonade.

And later on in life, when on several occasions I happened to drink champagne that was as flat and tasteless as weak lemonade, I would think back to this particular evening and reflect on the great if hardheaded wisdom of nature, which strives in everything for balance and equilibrium. For there is no such thing in this world as getting something for nothing; and if on occasion you are lucky enough to drink lemonade which reminds you of champagne, then sooner or later you will have to drink champagne which reminds you of lemonade.

Such is the sad but apparently inevitable logic of life. And perhaps even sadder than the logic itself is the fact that it is inevitable.

VIII

They say that even a stone can be worn away by drops of water. How much more so, by Platon Samsonovich! And already the agricultural administration office had agreed to set aside the necessary funds for the purchase of some Tadzhik goats; and already Platon Samsonovich—unwilling to let things run their official course—had sent off a letter to our Tadzhik colleagues, informing them of the upcoming transaction; and already they had written back, letting him know that they had heard about our interesting undertaking and had been planning to acquire some goatibexes of their own; and already they had agreed to an exchange of animals and were planning to carry on their own breeding experiments simultaneously with ours; and already Platon Samsonovich had gone off to the experimental farm to persuade the breeding specialist to accept an allotment of long-haired Tadzhik goats. But just at this point the storm broke. And it broke on the very day when Platon Samsonovich was due back from the experimental farm.

On this same day one of the Moscow papers printed an article ridiculing certain unwarranted innovations in the agricultural field. Our republic was found to be particularly at fault for what was described as our "ill-advised promotion of the goatibex." The article even called into question the genius of a certain well-known Moscow scientist whose experiments, it seemed, had proved something less than a complete success.*

Normally the Moscow papers didn't arrive until evening or even the next day, but on this occasion we learned of the article's

---

* Another reference to Lysenko. (Trans.)

contents on the same morning it was published. News of this sort always travels quickly.

I had never seen Avtandil Avtandilovich in such a state. He made several trips to regional Party headquarters in the course of the day and also placed a call to Party headquarters in the district where the experimental farm was located. Here he was informed that Platon Samsonovich had already boarded the bus and was on his way back to the city. The bus was scheduled to arrive at three p.m., and the editor called a general staff meeting for that hour.

By three o'clock we had all assembled in the editor's office. Since the bus stop happened to be located right across the street, everyone tried to sit next to the window in order to catch a glimpse of Platon Samsonovich as he got off the bus.

All of us were in a state bordering on nervous exaltation. Platon Samsonovich was the only one who had wholeheartedly supported the goatibex, and we all knew that the main blow would fall on him. And like a man who has just found some snug, protected spot in which to wait out a storm, each of us experienced a delightful sensation of warmth and well-being.

Avtandil Avtandilovich sat apart from the rest of us, gazing somewhere off into space. Before him lay a typewritten copy of the article, which he had apparently obtained from the wire service. It was the first time he had ever forgotten to turn off the fan and now, caught in the fast-moving current of air, the pages of the threatening article seemed to quiver and squirm with impatience.

On two separate occasions our staff humorist got up from his seat and walked past the editor as if to examine the map of Abkhazia which hung on the wall behind his desk. Although we all realized that he would hardly be able to decipher anything on the article's rippling pages, especially from behind Avtandil Avtandilovich's back, still we tried to signal him by means of various facial contortions to let us in on the article's contents. He, in turn, would grimace something to the effect that this was going to be an explosion to end all explosions.

With a mere nod of the head and without even bothering to turn around, Avtandil Avtandilovich ordered the staff humorist back to his seat.

Finally the bus drew up to the stop and we all crowded around the window to catch a glimpse of Platon Samsonovich.

Having for some reason assumed that he would be the first to get off, we were suddenly taken aback to see a hunting dog leap through the bus door. And following right behind was the hunter himself with a whole bevy of quail hanging from his belt. He walked away from the bus with the cheerfully lumbering gait of a man weighed down with success. I wistfully envied both man and dog.

And elderly peasant woman with a basket of walnuts got off the bus and started across the street in the middle of the block. A traffic policeman blew his whistle, but instead of stopping, she began to run, spilling her walnuts on the way. She kept on running until she had reached the other side of the street.

Platon Samsonovich was one of the last to get off. He stood for a moment beside the bus, his jacket hanging limply from one shoulder. Then he suddenly started off in the opposite direction from the newspaper office.

"He's walking away," someone was the first to gasp.

"What do you mean, walking away?" asked Avtandil Avtandilovich in a threatening tone.

"I'll go after him," cried the humorist, dashing toward the door.

"Be sure you don't tell him anything!" the editor shouted after him.

The rest of us stood by the window, not letting Platon Samsonovich out of our sight. With his jacket still slung over his shoulder he made his way slowly across the street. Having reached the other side, he suddenly halted by a soda water stand.

"He's stopping for soda water," someone noted in surprise, and we all burst out laughing.

The humorist came running out to the street and made his way to the nearest intersection. Raising one hand to shade his eyes from the sun, he began looking around in every direction. He didn't notice Platon Samsonovich, however, because another customer had come up to the stand and temporarily blocked him from view.

The humorist stood at the corner for several seconds, peering anxiously about. Then, beginning to panic, he dashed across the street and continued walking in the direction of the sea. We watched with eager curiosity as he began to approach the soda water stand. But his gaze was fixed so resolutely ahead that he walked right by without even noticing Platon Samsonovich. Once again we all burst out laughing. But just at this moment Platon Samsonovich must have hailed him, for he wheeled around in surprise. He addressed a few words to Platon Samsonovich and then, motioning in the direction of the office, quickly moved on. Knowing that we were watching him from the window, he undoubtedly felt self-conscious and wanted to have as little contact with Platon Samsonovich as possible.

In the meantime all of the remaining passengers had left the bus. And now as Platon Samsonovich was making his way back to the office, the bus driver suddenly darted out into the street and began retrieving the walnuts dropped by the peasant woman. When he had gathered up every last one of them, he got back into the bus and drove off.

After what seemed like an interminable wait, Platon Samsonovich opened the office door and walked in. He greeted us with a nod and sat down. His face wore a look of gloomy concentration, and even from the way he was perched on the edge of his chair, one could tell that he knew everything. Or perhaps I only imagine this in retrospect.

"Well, did you arrange everything with the breeding specialist?" the editor asked calmly.

Platon Samsonovich's tightly pressed lips began to tremble.

"Avtandil Avtandilovich," he said in a hollow voice as he rose half stooping from his chair. "I know everything…"

"Well, who told you, I'd like to know," asked the editor, now glancing at the humorist. The humorist threw up his hands in protest, then froze in position as if awaiting his fate.

"They reported it on the radio this morning," said Platon Samsonovich, continuing to stand in the same half-stooping position.

"So you're in the forefront here too," the editor joked gloomily, trying to hide his disappointment at not being the first to break the news.

The editor gazed coldly at Platon Samsonovich, and as the seconds passed, it was as if the distance between them had increased to the point where he almost ceased to recognize him. Under the weight of this gaze Platon Samsonovich seemed to grow even more stooped.

"Have a seat," said Avtandil Avtandilovich, addressing him in the tone reserved for chance visitors to the office.

In a clear, ringing voice the editor now began reading the article aloud. And as he read, gradually warming to his subject, he would occasionally cast a glance at Platon Samsonovich.

At first he seemed to include himself along with the rest of us in his recitation of our common errors and excesses. But as he kept on reading, the note of pathos in his voice continued to rise until suddenly it began to appear as if it were he himself, along with various other comrades, who had detected these errors. And by the time he finished, the tone of his voice had blended so well with that of the article in its rapid transitions from anger to irony that one might have imagined that it was he alone, without the help of any comrades, who had first noticed our mistakes and brought them boldly into the open.

Finally Avtandil Avtandilovich put down the article and declared the matter open for discussion. He spoke first and, to give him his due, he did criticize himself along with everyone else. For although he had in fact tried to call a halt to the ill-advised promotion of the goatibex (and for this very reason had insisted on printing the livestock expert's critical commentary, if only in the "Laughing at the Skeptics" column), still, his efforts in this direction had been insufficiently energetic and for this he must take at least part of the blame.

The humorist, who had been fidgeting impatiently all the while, took the floor immediately after Avtandil Avtandilovich and reminded us that in his satiric sketch about the man who had defaulted in his alimony payments, he too had tried to make a veiled criticism of the ill-advised promotion of the goatibex. But not only had Platon Samsonovich ignored his criticism—he had even tried to malign him.

"Malign you?" suddenly exclaimed Platon Samsonovich, gazing gloomily at the humorist.

"Yes, politically!" the latter firmly asserted, gazing back at him with the eyes of a man who has once and for all thrown off the chains of his bondage.

"You're exaggerating," interjected Avtandil Avtandilovich in conciliatory fashion. He did not like broad generalizations unless he was the one to make them.

136

Avtandil Avtandilovich now proceeded to raise the question of Platon Samsonovich's family life, which had inevitably suffered from the ill-advised promotion of the goatibex.

"His estrangement from the economic realities of collective farm life gradually led to an estrangement from his own family," the editor summarized. "And this is quite understandable, for having lost all criteria for truth, he came away with an inflated sense of his own importance."

After all of the staff members had voiced their individual support of his criticisms, Avtandil Avtandilovich took the floor once again—this time urging us to bear in mind that Platon Samsonovich was an old and experienced newspaper man who, for all his mistakes, was nonetheless devoted heart and soul to our common cause. Here too the staff was in complete agreement, and someone even quoted the saying to the effect that old horses shouldn't be put out to pasture.

The humorist, once again unable to restrain himself, now broke in to remind us that such excesses were all too typical of Platon Samsonovich. Several years before, for example, he had tried to develop a new method for catching fish. His idea was to run high-frequency electric currents through the water, thus encouraging the fish to collect in one particular area, away from the electric currents. But what had actually happened was that the fish had left the bay and might never have returned, had his experiments been allowed to continue.

"That wasn't the way it was supposed to work, you've got it all wrong," Platon Samsonovich was about to object, but by this time everyone was too tired to listen to technical details of an old experiment.

As the individual most sensitive to the winds of change, the head of the propaganda section was appointed to replace Platon Samsonovich as head of the agricultural section. In order to make his transition as easy as possible, Platon Samsonovich was to be kept on in the capacity of literary assistant. He was also given an official reprimand. For the time being the editor decided to take no further measures against him, though only on condition that he return to his family and enroll in night school at the beginning of the fall semester. Platon Samsonovich had never been to college.

"And by the way, be sure you get rid of that goatibex horn," instructed the editor as we were beginning to leave the room.

"The horn?" echoed Platon Samsonovich, his Adam's apple jerking convulsively as he spoke.

"Yes, the horn," repeated Avtandil Avtandilovich. "I don't ever want to see it again."

A few minutes later I saw Platon Samsonovich walk out of the building with the goatibex horn wrapped carelessly in a sheet of newspaper. As I pictured him returning to his solitary apartment with his solitary horn—now all that remained of his grand design— I felt a sudden wave of pity. But what was I to do? I could not bring myself to comfort him, nor would I have succeeded had I tried.

The Moscow article was reprinted in our paper, and the section dealing with the ill-advised promotion of the goatibex was put in italics for special emphasis. In the same issue there appeared an editorial entitled "The Ill-Advised Promotion of the Goatibex," which contained a critical evaluation of our paper's recent performance, and especially that of the agricultural section. The editorial also made reference to certain university lecturers who, without bothering to find out what it was all about, had thoughtlessly offered their services to the propagandizing of this new and as yet insufficiently investigated experiment.

While the writers of the editorial were obviously alluding to Vakhtang Bochua, they hesitated to attack him directly, since only a week before, he had presented the local historical museum with a valuable collection of Caucasian minerals.

Naturally, Vakhtang had seen to it that his gift did not go unnoticed. He had phoned in to the newspaper and asked us to have someone attend the presentation ceremony. The assignment was given to the staff photographer, who did indeed produce a memorable photograph of the occasion. Looking for all the world like a repentant pirate, Vakhtang was shown handing over his treasures to the shy museum director.

And now, only one short week after this magnificent display of altruism it seemed somehow inappropriate to bring up his name in connection with the goatibex.

Subsequent issues of the paper featured carefully screened reader responses to the attack on the goatibex. Here I should add that one of our staff members paid a special visit to the stubborn livestock expert in order to persuade him to write a long article against the goatibexation of the livestock industry. But the stubborn livestock expert remained true to character and flatly refused to write any such article. Apparently the subject no longer interested him.

After our publication of the Moscow article we were besieged with phone calls. Someone from the trade office, for example, called in to get our advice on what should be done about the name of the soft drink pavilion "The Watering Place of the Goatibex." We also began to receive warning calls to the effect that in some kolkhozes goatibexes were being slaughtered. In this connection we advised the interested parties to avoid rushing from one extreme to another; instead they should see to it that the goatibexes were treated like any other animal and quickly integrated into the collective farm herd.

After consulting with the rest of us as to what to advise the trade office people, Avtandil Avtandilovich decided that here too there was no need to go to extremes. Rather than destroy the pavilion sign completely, they should merely eliminate the first syllable of the word "goatibex" as quietly and inconspicuously as possible, thus transforming the pavilion into "The Watering Place of the Ibex"—a much more romantic name as it seemed to me.

While the sign on the pavilion itself was quickly altered according to Avtandil Avtandilovich's specifications, the neon sign above the pavilion proved to be somewhat of a problem. In fact, every night for a whole month afterward the letters of the old name, "The Watering Place of the Goatibex," winked down impudently from on high. Thus one might have supposed that the watering place was frequented by ibexes during the day, while at night the stubborn goatibexes still held sway.

Certain members of the local intelligentsia began congregating in this spot for the express purpose of gazing up at the neon sign. For them it seemed to contain a hint of the liberals' struggle against something or other, while at the same time offering concrete proof of the dogmatists' wicked intransigence.

One evening as I happened to be entering the café next door, I myself saw some of these freethinkers gathered in a large if unobtrusive group outside the pavilion.

"There's more to this than meets the eye," declared one of them with a slight nod in the direction of the neon sign.

"Spit in my eye if this is going to be the end of it," said another.

"My friends," interrupted a prudent voice, "everything you say is true; still, you shouldn't stare so openly at the sign. Just take a quick look and walk past."

"Who does he think he is?!" protested the first one. "If I feel like looking, I'll go ahead and look. This isn't the old days."

"No, but someone might get the wrong idea," said the voice of prudence, peering cautiously around him. Then, noticing me, he immediately stopped short and added: "Well, as I was saying, the criticism has come at just the right time."

They all looked over in my direction and, as if by command, began moving toward the café, now vehemently gesticulating as they continued their argument in barely audible tones.

During this same period I received a phone call from the business manager of the Municipal Opera and Choral Society, who wanted my advice as to what should be done about the goat-ibex song, which was still being performed by the tobacco factory choir as well as by several soloists.

"You see, I do have a financial plan to fulfill," he said in an apologetic voice, "and the song is very popular..., and though its popularity may not be a good thing, as I can now appreciate, still..."

I decided that it wouldn't hurt to consult Avtandil Avtandilovich on this particular matter.

"Please hold on for just a minute," I said to the business manager, and putting down the receiver, I set off for the editor's office.

After hearing me out, Avtandil Avtandilovich declared that any choral performances of the goatibex song were absolutely out of the question.

"And besides, the members of that choir are no more tobacco workers than I am," he added abruptly. "But as far as the soloists are concerned, I think it's all right for them to sing it, as long as they give the right interpretation to the words. The main thing now," he concluded, switching on the fan, "is to avoid rushing from one extreme to another. Just tell him that."

140

I conveyed the contents of our conversation to the guardian of the Municipal Opera and Choral Society, after which he hung up—rather pensively as it seemed to me.

Platon Samsonovich had not come to work that day. On the following day his wife appeared in his place and marched straight into the editor's office. Several minutes later the editor summoned the chairman of the trade union committee, who subsequently told the rest of us what had happened. It seemed that upon hearing of the goatibex's fate, Platon Samsonovich's wife had gone to visit her husband in his solitary apartment and had found him lying in bed, the victim either of some sort of nervous disorder resulting from physical exhaustion or of physical exhaustion resulting from some sort of nervous disorder. In any case, they had now become reconciled once and for all, and Platon Samsonovich's wife had rejoined her husband in the old apartment, leaving the new apartment to their grown children.

"There, you see," said Avtandil Avtandilovich in a conciliatory tone, "healthy criticism actually contributes to the well-being of the family."

"Well, the criticism may be healthy, but I've got a very sick man on my hands," she replied.

"Well, there we can be of some help," Avtandil Avtandilovich assured her, at the same time instructing the chairman of the trade union committee to obtain a sick pass for the ailing Platon Samsonovich.

Whether due to a quirk of fate or to some quirk of the committee chairman, Platon Samsonovich was sent off to a mountain health resort which until very recently had been named in honor of the goatibex. This particular resort, I might add, is one of the best in our Republic and is usually booked solid for months in advance.

About two weeks later, when the last volleys of goatibex counterpropaganda had finally died down, when the animals themselves had been utterly repulsed and their scattered and isolated numbers finally reconciled to joining the ranks of the collective farm herd—just at this time there took place in our city a one-day agricultural conference attended by our region's most successful collective farmers. The conference had been convened to celebrate our Republic's overfulfillment of its tea production quotas for the year—an event of no small importance since tea is our major crop.

Not surprisingly, Illarion Maksimovich's kolkhoz at Walnut Springs numbered among our region's most successful tea-raising collectives, and during the recess following the morning business session I happened to catch sight of Illarion Maksimovich himself. He was seated with the agronomist and Gogola at a small table in the conference hall restaurant. The two men were drinking beer, while Gogola was munching a pastry as she gazed wide-eyed at the other women in the room.

Just the day before, our paper had done a feature story on the tea growers of Walnut Springs, so I felt no qualms about approaching them. We exchanged greetings and they asked me to join them.

The agronomist looked the same as ever, but on the chairman's face I noticed an expression of restrained irony—the same sort of expression one sees on a peasant's face when he is forced out of politeness to listen to a city person hold forth on the subject of agriculture. It was only when the chairman turned to Gogola that his eyes showed any signs of life.

"Would you like another pastry, Gogola?"

"No thanks," she replied absentmindedly as she continued to gaze at the women, all of whom had donned their party best for the occasion.

"Oh, come on, just one more," said the chairman, trying to coax her.

"I don't want another pastry, but a lemonade would be real nice," she finally consented.

"A bottle of lemonade," said Illarion Maksimovich, addressing the waitress.

"Well, are you happy that they've called off the goatibex?" I asked the chairman when he had finished filling each of our glasses with beer.

"It's a fine undertaking," he replied, "but there's only one thing I'm afraid of..."

"What's that?" I asked, eyeing him with curiosity.

He drained the contents of his glass and set it back on the table.

"If they've called off the goatibex," he said pensively, as if gazing into the future, "that means they'll be thinking up something new, and for our climatic conditions..."

142

"I know," I interrupted, "for your climatic conditions it wouldn't be appropriate."

"That's it exactly," confirmed the chairman, now completely serious.

"I really don't think you have to worry," I said, trying to sound as reassuring as possible.

"Well, let's hope not," he said slowly and then added: "But if they've called off the goatibex, there's bound to be something new—though just what, I don't know."

"And what's happened to your goatibex?" I asked.

"He's joined the collective herd and is being treated like any other animal," replied the chairman as if talking about something very remote, which no longer posed a threat.

The bell rang, and we returned to the conference hall. I said good-bye to them and stationed myself at the door so that I could make a quick exit later on. I was supposed to return to the office and write up my report as soon as the concert was over.

Pata Pataraya's Caucasian dancers were the first to appear and, as always, these agile, light-footed performers were greeted with thunderous applause.

They were called back for several encores, and now appearing on stage along with them was Pata Pataraya himself—a slim elderly man with a resilient step. Heartened by the audience's enthusiastic response, he finally treated us to his famed "knee flight," dating back to the nineteen-thirties.

In performing this *tour de force* he would come flying onto the stage at lightning speed, suddenly drop down on his knees and then, with arms outstretched and head held proudly erect, he would slide on his knees diagonally across the stage as if making a beeline toward the loge reserved for top government officials. But at the very last second, as the audience sat paralyzed, half expecting him to topple into the orchestra, Pata Pataraya would jump up as if released by a spring and begin whirling in the air like a black tornado.

The spectators went wild.

When Pata Pataraya and his dancers had finally left the stage, the mistress of ceremonies announced:

"A *chonguri** trio will perform a song without words."

---

* An ancient Caucasian stringed instrument somewhat smaller than the guitar. (Trans.)

Three girls in long white dresses and white kerchiefs walked onto the brightly lit stage. They sat down and began tuning their *chonguris*, listening attentively and casting shy glances at one another. Then one of them gave a signal and they began to play. Their voices immediately took up the melody on the strings and they began singing in imitation of the mountaineer's old-fashioned song without words.

The melody seemed strangely familiar and suddenly I realized that it was the former goatibex song, though now at a much slower tempo. A gasp of recognition passed through the hall, and glancing over in Illarion Maksimovich's direction, I noticed that an expression of restrained irony still lingered on his broad face. Perhaps this was the expression he always assumed when visiting the city, and most likely it would not change until the moment of his departure. Gogola was sitting next to the chairman, her slim, pretty neck craned forward as she gazed up at the stage like one bewitched. And next to her, the sleepy agronomist sat dozing in his chair like General Kutuzov* at a military staff meeting.

The three *chonguri* players received even more applause than Pata Pataraya and were forced to sing two encores of their song without words—a song which for this particular audience had all the sweetness of forbidden fruit.

And although the fruit itself had proved extremely bitter—as no one knew better than the individuals in this hall—and although they were all very glad that it had been forbidden, nonetheless it was pleasant to savor its sweetness, if only the sweetness of its interdiction. Such, apparently, is the nature of man and such it is likely to remain.

---

* Russia's commanding general during the Napoleonic invasion of 1812 and a figure well-known to readers of *War and Peace*. (Trans.)

Life in our editorial office had returned to normal. Platon Samsonovich had come back from his mountain resort completely restored to health, and on the day following his return he had asked me to go fishing with him. I was flattered by his invitation and accepted with pleasure.

As I have already mentioned, Platon Samsonovich was one of the most experienced fishermen along our shores, and if the fish didn't seem to be biting in one spot, he would say to me:

"I know another spot..."

And I would start rowing toward the other spot. But if they didn't seem to be biting here either, he would say:

"I know a completely different spot..."

And I would start rowing toward the completely different spot. But if even here they didn't seem to be biting, then he would lie down in the stern and say:

"You might as well head back to shore; the fish have gone out to deeper waters."

And I would head back to shore, for in such matters Platon Samsonovich's word was law.

But this sort of thing happened rarely, and on this occasion, as was usually the case, we made a good haul. Platon Samsonovich was especially successful—he being one of those fisherman who would throw out ten lines at a time. His lines would be attached to flexible poles, and as the latter hung suspended over the side of the boat, he would somehow manage to keep up with the nibbles on each line without getting them crossed. And whenever he would give one of his lines a gentle tug, lifting it slightly and at the same time listening intently to what was happening down below, it was as if he were some fabulous puppeteer manipulating the strings of this underwater kingdom.

After we had tied up at the pier and come ashore, I feasted my eyes once again on Platon Samsonovich's catch. Along with the other, more common varieties of fish flapping in his net, there was a beautiful sea cock—a prize species of the Black Sea and one that I myself had never succeeded in catching.

"Not only are you an expert, you're lucky as well," I commented enviously.

"Oh, by the way, I made an interesting discovery when I was fishing up in the mountains," he said after a short pause.

We were walking along next to the sea wall—he with a whole netful of wet fish and I with my more modest catch in a small string bag.

"What sort of discovery," I asked without much curiosity.

"Well, when I was looking for trout up there along the banks of the Upper Kodor, I just happened upon a fantastic cave..."

Something in his voice put me on guard. I stole a glance at his eyes and saw that once again they had their old, feverish glitter.

"There are thousands of such caves up in the mountains," I sharply interjected.

"Not at all," he replied heatedly, his eyes lighting up with a harsh, unpleasant glitter. "That cave had an unusual array of stalactites and stalagmites; they were like clusters of flowers of all different colors... I brought back a whole suitcaseful of samples."

"And what are you going to do with them?" I asked, taking as distant a tone as possible.

"I want to get some Party officials interested in this... This is no mere cave, it's an underground palace, a fairy tale, an absolute gold mine..."

Suddenly his face had a new, youthful look, and I realized that all the energy he had managed to store up during his stay in the mountains would now be expended on this cave.

"There are thousands of such caves up there in the mountains," I dully repeated.

"If a cableway were installed, tourists could be whisked up to this underground palace straight from their steamships—and along the way they could take in the view of the Kodor Delta and the surrounding mountains..."

"That's a distance of over a hundred kilometers," I interrupted, "and who's going to give you the money for a project like that?"

"It would pay for itself! It would pay for itself in no time!" he joyfully exclaimed, and dropping his fishnet onto the wall, he continued: "Tourists will come flocking by the thousands from all over the world. Straight from the boat to the cave..."

"Not to mention the fact that one shepherd will be able to tend two thousand goatibexes," I broke in facetiously.

"What does this have to do with goatibexes?" he asked in genuine surprise. "It's tourism that's being promoted now. Did you know that Italy lives off its tourist trade?"

"Well, okay," I said, "I'm going to stop for a cup of coffee. You can do as you please."

"Wait a minute," he called after me as I began walking away. I sensed that he was trying to involve me and I was determined not to let it happen.

"You see, I left the suitcase with the samples in the baggage room at the station," he said shyly.

"No, I don't see," I replied coolly.

"Well, you can imagine, if my wife sees those stalactites and stalagmites, she'll immediately start pestering me."

"What has that got to do with me?" I asked, suddenly realizing what lay behind his fishing invitation.

"We'll go and pick up the suitcase, and I'll leave it at your place just for the time being..."

Having just returned from a day's fishing, I had no desire to traipse across town to the railroad station, and I quickly replied:

"Okay, but it'll have to wait till tomorrow. Your stalactites won't spoil overnight, I trust."

"Don't be silly!" he exclaimed. "Why, they last for thousands of years—and these particular ones have an amazingly rare coloration, as you'll see for yourself tomorrow."

"Well, okay, till tomorrow," I said.

"Good-bye," he mumbled with a faraway look in his eyes as he carelessly picked up his netful of beautiful fish.

147

I hadn't taken more than a few steps, when he stopped me again. I turned around.

"Don't say anything about the cave for the time being," he said, pressing a finger to his lips.

"Okay, I won't," I replied and quickly walked off in the direction of the café.

It was evening—one of those marvelous, still evenings typical of early fall in our area. The sun was sinking slowly into the sea, and the western end of the bay had become a mass of flaming gold. Toward the east the gold was gradually fading, taking on first lilac, then ashen hues. Still farther to the east both sea and shore had already blurred into a grayish-blue haze.

My thoughts returned to Platon Samsonovich. It occurred to me that he and others like him represented a new and strange type of innovator (or inventor or entrepreneur—call him what you will) typical of our era. Since it was the government itself which supported him, he could never go completely bankrupt, no matter how many times he might fail. And for this very reason, not only was his source of funds virtually inexhaustible, but his enthusiasm as well.

The café was filled with the usual old-timers, who sat drinking their coffee in small gulps, quietly savoring old memories. In one corner, where several tables had been pushed together, the young men were conversing with the noisy exuberance of youth.

I sat down at one of the tables, hanging my string bag on the back of my chair.

"Sweet or semisweet?" asked the waiter, nodding his head with the benign expression of some Oriental wise man. As he caught sight of my fish, a look of approval flashed across his round face which seemed to have been browned by sun and coffee alike.

"Semisweet," I replied as usual.

I felt pleasantly exhausted after all my rowing, and at the moment I could imagine nothing more appealing than a cup of hot Turkish coffee topped with its fine brown foam.

So it is that I bring to a close my true story of the goatibex. And if I purposely omit any further reference to the girl whom I met on the pier, I do so not only to prove how elusive and self-controlled I can be, but also for the simple reason that her vacation had come to an end and she had already returned home to resume her studies. More to the point, she belongs to another chapter in my life—one which I'm happy to say has absolutely no connection with goatibexes.

The southern night came on quickly. I looked up at the sky, trying to locate the constellation which had once reminded me of the goatibex. But ever since that evening with Valiko, try as I might, I had never found anything even slightly resembling it. So too on this occasion: the sky was full of constellations, but the goatibex was nowhere in sight.

I sat there sipping my coffee, and each time I raised the cup to my lips and sucked in a hot, thick mouthful, I would feel at my elbow the gentle pressure of my string bag full of fish. It was as if my own dog were sitting behind me, thrusting his cold, moist nose into my elbow as a subtle reminder of his presence. The sensation was a pleasant one, and I didn't change my position until I had drained the contents of my cup.

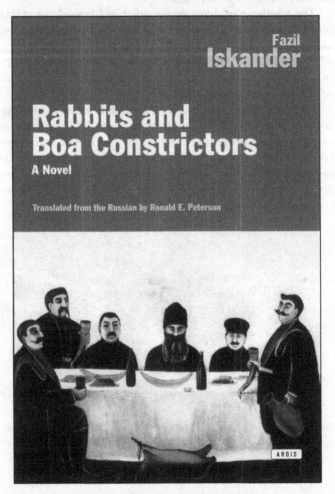

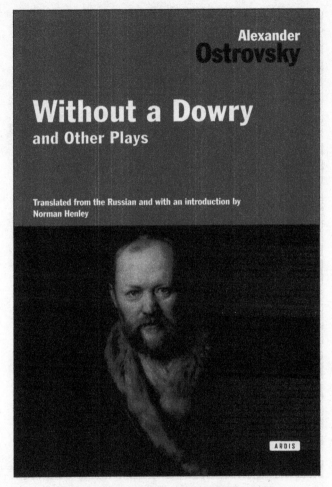

Alexander
Ostrovsky

Without a Dowry
and Other Plays

Translated from the Russian and with an introduction by
Norman Henley

ARDIS

WITHOUT A DOWRY AND OTHER PLAYS
ALEXANDER OSTROVSKY
Translated from the Russian and with an introduction by Norman Henley
978-1-4683-0858-7 • PB • $21.95

CONTACT SALES@OVERLOOKNY.COM FOR OUR MOST RECENT ARDIS CATALOG

THE OVERLOOK PRESS
New York, NY
www.overlookpress.com
www.ardisbooks.com

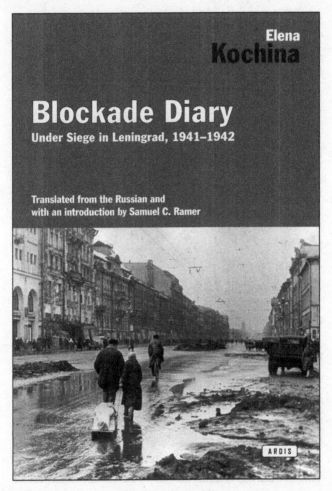

Elena
Kochina

Blockade Diary
Under Siege in Leningrad, 1941–1942

Translated from the Russian and
with an introduction by Samuel C. Ramer

ARDIS

BLOCKADE DIARY
ELENA KOCHINA
Translated from the Russian and with an introduction by Samuel C. Ramer
978-1-4683-0969-0 • PB • $16.95

THE OVERLOOK PRESS
New York, NY
www.overlookpress.com
www.ardisbooks.com

RED SPECTRES
RUSSIAN GOTHIC TALES FROM THE 20TH CENTURY
Selected and translated with an introduction by Muireann Maguire
978-1-4683-0348-3 • PB • $25.95

THE OVERLOOK PRESS
New York, NY
www.overlookpress.com
www.ardisbooks.com

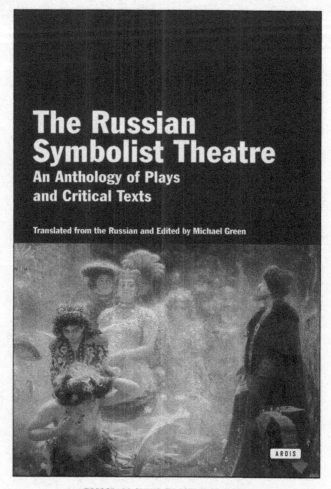

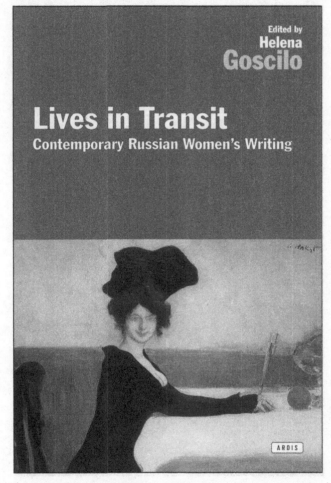

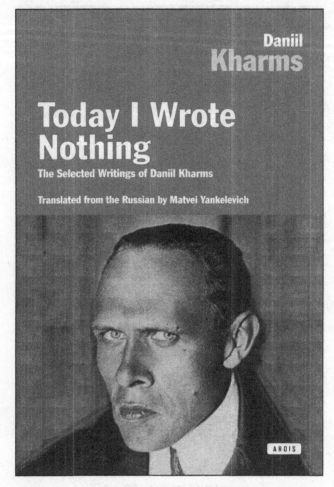

vladislav khodasevich
selected poems

translated from the russian by peter daniels
introduction by michael wachtel
bilingual edition

OVERLOOK / ARDIS

VLADISLAVE KHODASEVICH SELECTED POEMS
Translated from the Russian by Peter Daniels
Introduction by Michael Wachtel
978-1-4683-0810-5 • HC • $27.95

THE OVERLOOK PRESS
New York, NY
www.overlookpress.com
www.ardisbooks.com

ARDIS

Publishers of Russian Literature

Nikolai Evreinov
Theater as Life

J.A.E. Curtis
Manuscripts Don't Burn
Mikhail Bulgakov: A Life in Letters and Diaries

Lev Razgon
True Stories

Carl Proffer
Russian Romantic Prose
An Anthology

M.E. Saltykov
The Golovlyov Family

M. Kuzmin
Selected Prose & Poetry
Of Mikhail Kuzmin

Anna Akhmatova
My Half Century

Fyodor Dostoevsky
The Crocodile

Boris Pilnyak
Mahogany
& Other Stories

Helena Goscilo
Lives in Transit
Contemporary Russian Women's Writing

Alexander Pushkin
Eugene Onegin

Fyodor Dostoevsky
Poor Folk

Marina Tsvetaeva
Poem of the End

Anna Akhmatova
Selected Poems

Fyodor Dostoevsky
The Double
Two Version

Mikhail Bulgakov
Notes on the Cuff
& Other Stories

Alexander Pushkin
Pushkin Threefold

Vla... Nabokov
The Song of Igor's Campaign

Mikhail Bulgakov
Diaboliad
& Other Stories

Mikhail Lermontov
A Hero of Our Time

Fyodor Sologub
The Petty Demon

Marina Tsvetaeva
A Captive Spirit
Selected Prose

Yury Olesha
Envy

Osip Mandelstam
Critical Prose and Letters

OVERLOOK DUCKWORTH
New York • London
www.overlookpress.com
www.ducknet.co.uk
www.ardisbooks.com